The Proof that Ghosts Exist

The Ghosthunters

BOOK ONE

The Proof that Ghosts Exist

by Carol Matas & Perry Nodelman

KEY PORTER BOOKS

Library and Archives Canada Cataloguing in Publication

Matas, Carol, 1949-
 The proof that ghosts exist / Carol Matas & Perry Nodelman.

(Ghosthunters)
ISBN 978-1-55470-014-1

I. Nodelman, Perry II. Title. III. Series: Matas, Carol, 1949- .
Ghosthunters.

PS8576.A7994P76 2008   jC813'.54   C2007-906679-8

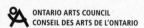

ONTARIO ARTS COUNCIL
CONSEIL DES ARTS DE L'ONTARIO

The publisher gratefully acknowledges the support of the Canada Council for the Arts and the Ontario Arts Council for its publishing program. We acknowledge the support of the Government of Ontario through the Ontario Media Development Corporation's Ontario Book Initiative.

We acknowledge the financial support of the Government of Canada through the Book Publishing Industry Development Program (BPIDP) for our publishing activities.

Key Porter Books Limited
Six Adelaide Street East, Tenth Floor
Toronto, Ontario
Canada M5C 1H6

www.keyporter.com

Text design: Alison Carr
Electronic formatting: Alison Carr

Printed and bound in Canada

08 09 10 11 12 5 4 3 2 1

To David Bennett, with thanks for letting us borrow the ghosts of his past, and for providing us with the evidence.

Prologue

"*The existence of ghosts must be provable.*"

"*But,*" *he wrote, underlining the word so forcefully that the point of the pen nearly cut through the paper,* "*the evidence must be presented with a rigour impeccable enough to persuade even the most skeptical of scientists. The following are documented case histories that might be the basis for serious scientific consideration.*"

He put down the ballpoint and rifled through the large stack of papers piled on the handsome carved oak desk, searching for a document he knew was there somewhere. With his wrinkled brow and his pale skin, he looked older than his thirty-five years. But his long, shoulder-length hair was still a bright carrot-red, and the eyes behind his round, steel-rimmed glasses were an intense blue. He wore an open-necked purple paisley shirt beneath a crumpled ivory linen jacket.

A fire burnt cheerily in the grate and he was glad of that, for although it was summer, the breeze from the window was cool. He raised his eyes and took a quick glance toward the window behind him. The trees were in full green. A fine English summer morning. Perhaps when he'd finished a bit more work he'd take a walk by the river.

But wait. There was something strange about the trees. Something he hadn't noticed right away because he hadn't really been paying much attention. He turned and looked again.

He took off his glasses, rubbed his eyes, and put the glasses on again.

It wasn't possible! The sturdy English oaks and beeches that towered over the Botanical Gardens opposite his window were gone, and in their place stood tall pines. In fact, the entire Botanical Gardens had vanished into thin air!

It didn't look like Oxford at all. It looked like some kind of northern forest—in Scandinavia, perhaps, or Northern Russia.

What was happening? Where was he?

CHAPTER ONE
The Ghost of a Storm

A dark cloud swooped in from nowhere just as the car took the turn-off marked Falcon Lake. For a brief moment the cloud enveloped the car. Thunder crashed, lightning flashed, and rain smashed against the windshield. Molly and Adam shivered—both at the same time—and Charlie, the dog, whined. Their father, Tim, swore. And then, as suddenly as it had appeared, the storm was gone.

Molly tried to shake off the very bad feeling that had surrounded her like the cloud had surrounded the car. "Well, at least we're on our way," she said.

"Yeah," Adam replied glumly. "On our way and it's going to be a disaster. Think about Dad's cooking, and remember—there's the leeches."

Molly grimaced. As much as she hated to admit it, her younger brother had a point. The food would be bad, the leeches would be, well, leechy, and there sure wasn't going to be all that family togetherness stuff they'd been promised. At least not to begin with. But that was exactly what was so amazing! That Dad, Adam, herself, and Charlie were heading off to the lake even though Mom wasn't coming. She'd actually allowed them to go without her.

Charlie, asleep at Molly's feet, whimpered again. Perhaps, Molly thought, he was having a nightmare about the vicious cat next door, or some snarling dog three times larger than himself. Charlie was big for a Wheaten Terrier, but that wasn't saying much. Or maybe he was just imagining the leftovers from Dad's so-called meals. Ugh.

Molly went over the morning's events in her mind. She had been so anxious to get out of the hot, sticky city that she'd gotten up bright-and-early to start packing the car. At about ten, with only the food left to pack, she'd gone into the kitchen to find her mom standing by the phone, a grim look on her face. That could only mean one thing: trouble.

"You should never answer that phone!" Molly exclaimed as her mother put the receiver back in its cradle.

"Not answering doesn't make the problem go away," her mom replied crisply.

That was when her dad had come in, shutting the door behind him to prevent any more mosquitoes from following. He took one look at his wife's face and his shoulders sagged.

"Don't tell me."

"The maintenance workers are threatening to go out," Mom said. "I have to be there."

And of course, she did have to be there. To Mom, the hospital was like another family—another family for her to love and protect and keep running smoothly, just the way she looked after her family at home.

"I knew it," said Adam, who'd been shovelling cereal into his mouth. "I hate that hospital. Although . . . ," he stopped and stared thoughtfully into space, "maybe it isn't the workers' fault. Maybe it's an alien species with ESP using thought control on them, just to stop us all from going to the lake so we can protect Dad—"

Adam stopped in mid-sentence and blushed, turning almost the same bright red as the hair he shared with his father. "Um, I mean, have fun together. Protecting our family health, like."

Molly snuck a look at her father, who was standing stock still in the middle of the kitchen, looking annoyed. Dad, Molly knew full well, was no fool. He knew *exactly* what Adam had been about to say. Dad's father, a professor at Oxford University in England, had dropped dead at his desk the day before his thirty-fifth birthday. So had his grandfather, a country parson, and possibly his great-grandfather as well. Rumour had it that even his great-great-grandfather had died the day before *his* thirty-fifth birthday, way back in the distant past. It seemed to be a bizarre, and very horrible, long-standing family tradition. And Dad was going to turn thirty-five tomorrow. Tomorrow!

While his doctors pronounced him fit and healthy, Mom, Molly, and Adam were more than a little panicked. That's why Mom had insisted on this trip to the lake—so they could all keep a close eye on him. And she had sworn Molly and Adam to secrecy about why they were really going. Still, Molly could tell Dad knew. And that he was annoyed about it. He refused to take the threat seriously.

"Nonsense, Adam," Dad said. He picked up a bag of washed fruit and stashed it in the cooler. "It's not a problem. Just because your mom has to stay here today doesn't mean the rest of us can't go."

Molly had waited, holding her breath. You could tell from the look on Mom's face that she was torn. All of them staying at home didn't really make sense. Mom knew she was going to be too busy to keep her eye on Dad anyway. Besides, if she did her job at the hospital well—and she always did—then she'd be out at the lake with them by evening at the latest. She'd just have to trust that, in the meantime, Molly and Adam could watch Dad for her. "You're right," she said, a tight smile crossing her face. "You should go ahead. I'll catch up with you as soon as I can." It was settled, then. Almost as soon as Mom had agreed to let them go, she dragged Adam and Molly out onto the back porch and swore them to secrecy. She told them that they had to watch Dad every moment and never let him out of their sight even for an instant. He wasn't to swim too hard or jog too far or lift anything too heavy. And, Mom said, she was going to call up Mrs. Rosen in the cottage next to theirs and ask her to keep an eye on things—and the McDermots from around the bay, and maybe the Park police, too. Mom wasn't taking any chances.

"Remember," she shouted as the car finally backed out of the driveway, "remember what I said, Molly."

After all that fuss and bother, Molly was not about to forget. But it was all so silly! Nothing was going to happen to Dad. It was just a big fuss over nothing.

A loud ringing interrupted Molly's thoughts. Dad's cell. He took one hand off the wheel and reached into his shirt pocket to get it.

"I wish," said Adam, "that you'd turn that thing off while you're driving."

Molly gave Adam one of her looks—the one that meant he was worrying too much. But Adam knew he wasn't worrying too much. He was just being realistic. He could picture it so clearly: Dad would be shouting into the phone at somebody back at the studio about what colour to paint the backgrounds or how much to spend on duct tape. He'd be so wrapped up in thinking about the documentary he was making he wouldn't even notice the giant bear that had suddenly stepped out onto the road right in front of the car. The car, after all, was now following a narrow road that hugged the lake and soon they would be on the gravel road that led to the cottage. Animals ran onto the road all the time—bears, deer, they'd even seen a wolf once. The car would slam right into the bear, or deer or wolf. There'd be gross pieces of some sort of animal splattered everywhere—not to mention pieces of Molly and Dad. And pieces of Adam. Anyway, Dad wouldn't reach his thirty-fifth birthday—and neither would Molly or Charlie. Or Adam. Who invented cell phones, anyway? What were they thinking? It must have been eco-terrorists trying to lower the population of car drivers.

"Yes," Dad said into the phone. "Tim Barnett here."

Adam had to admit that wayward animals weren't the biggest danger. The biggest danger was that it would be Mom again. She'd already called them twice in the hour-and-a-half since they'd left home—once, she said, to see if they'd remembered to bring the low-fat salad dressing, because Dad wasn't allowed the real stuff, and once to remind them to keep the garbage inside until just before the pick-up time, to keep the bears away. What was the point of her staying in the city if she was going to be calling every twenty seconds?

"He did what?" Dad said, his voice rising in anger. Maybe it wasn't Mom after all.

"No," Dad continued. "You deal with it. I'm on the way to the lake with the kids." He paused for a moment. "No," he said gruffly, "I'm turning my phone off as soon as I get there—and leaving it off. You'll have to handle it on your own. Just stick to the plan. You do have a copy of the plan, don't you? I left enough sheets for everybody." He listened for a moment, then nodded and said, "The plan. Remember the plan." Then he clicked the phone off, mumbling something under his breath so that Adam and Molly wouldn't hear. But that Adam did hear. Dad certainly had a large and interesting vocabulary! Adam had rarely heard a grown-up use language like that, only kids at school when the teachers weren't there.

"I hate that phone," said Molly. "We're not going back, are we?"

"Don't worry," said Dad. "I told them I was taking these two weeks before we start shooting in the Fort Garry Hotel no matter what. That's what I told them and that's what I meant. I'm staying with you guys and that's that."

And that was good, Adam thought. Really. It meant if the aliens landed Dad would be there to try to do something about it.

"Okay, folks," said Dad. "Here we are!"

The cottage! Molly's favourite place in the whole

world! She jumped out of the car, taking deep breaths of the wonderful lake air. It smelled so clean, so fresh! The cottage was just a short flight of steps down from the carport, nestled in a hill overlooking the lake, in a bay with five others.

Molly couldn't resist. She had to get inside right away and say hello to her room.

It was a small room with a single bed and a bookshelf under the window, and it had Wonder Woman curtains. Her mom's parents had put them up back when her mom was just a little girl and sleeping in that room herself. Mom had chosen the curtains, because Wonder Woman was her favourite character. "When I was young," Mom had giggled, "I just knew for sure that I was going to be Wonder Woman when I grew up."

Molly loved the fact that the curtains were still there, just like they always had been. And the bed was Mom's old bed, and most of the books on the shelves had been there ever since Molly could remember. There was Mom's battered old copy of *Ozma of Oz* and *The Road to Oz* and *The Secret Garden* and, of course, every Stephen King book ever written. Adam wasn't allowed to read those because he got nightmares, but Molly had read them all, putting each one back exactly where she had found it. Everything in its place, everything the way it always was and should be. It made Molly happy.

Ignoring her dad's order to carry something with her, she rushed down the steps, grabbed the key from under the big flowerpot beside the door, unlocked the cottage, and ran in, shouting over her shoulder.

"Don't worry about it," she called. "I'll get the stuff later. I have to go look at my room!"

CHAPTER TWO
Ghosts of the Past

"*I have to go look at my room!*"

The red-haired man sat up and listened. Who on earth was that? Things were getting stranger with every passing moment. The business of the trees had been just the beginning. When he'd gotten up to look out the window and investigate, he'd almost blacked out. He'd reached out to steady himself on the desk, and as soon as his fingers made contact with the wood, he'd felt fine. Once again, he'd started to move toward the window, but the feeling returned. After a few more experiments, he realized that he became dizzy every time he stepped away from the desk. It made no sense!

It reminded him of the vertigo he'd experienced that dark day—the day his father had died. Pops had seemed old to him then, but later, he'd realized that he'd only been thirty-five, a young man in his prime. Although Pops had strictly forbidden him from playing in the study, he'd been behind the curtains, conducting his usual game of "hide-and-hide" (when no one knew he was hiding) and he'd seen Pops screaming in horror until his heart gave way—scared to death.

And no one believed him.

He was just a child, after all, and he'd been frozen in fear himself—unable to help, too terrified by Pops' terror to even move. But there had been something. He'd seen something. And although he never knew what it was exactly, he felt sure it wasn't of this world. His mother and the doctors all used words like "trauma" and convinced him he'd imagined the entire thing. But he'd been fascinated, some might say obsessed, with the supernatural ever since.

And now something strange was happening to **him**—there was no doubt about it. But what? And who did that voice belong to?

Molly, Charlie at her heels, burst through the door and then, suddenly, stopped, unable to believe what she was seeing. What was going on?

Her bedroom was full of boxes! Some of them were open and filled with books and papers. Others were taped shut and stacked one on top of the other. Behind the boxes, she could see a desk, an old-fashioned wooden one.

The room was a mess. As her glance darted this way and that, trying to take it all in, she saw something else, too. The top of a head—a head covered with shoulder-length, carrot-red hair. Someone was in her room. A man. A pair of blue eyes gazed at her—a familiar pair of eyes.

"Dad?" It made no sense. How could he have gotten here before she did? Hadn't she left him sitting in the car? And . . . was he wearing a wig? Where did all that hair come from? He looked ridiculous, like some hippie from the ancient past. And he was staring at her intently—as if he was seeing a ghost or something.

As Molly gazed back at the eyes gazing at her, Charlie began barking frantically, jumping up and down as if he wanted to see over all the boxes to the figure beyond. Over his barking Molly heard a voice.

"Molly! Get in here this instant. I want all these frozen things put away right now, before they melt!"

It was Dad's voice, and it was coming from the kitchen.

Dad was in the kitchen. Then who—?

She turned back toward the desk. No one was there.

She was sure she'd seen Dad, but there wasn't anyone behind the desk now. There was nothing except all those messy boxes and books and things, whatever they were.

And whatever they were, they were very annoying. "My room! This is just plain wrong!" she said aloud, stamping her foot. With Charlie barking as if there were no tomorrow, she couldn't think straight!

"Charlie!" she scolded. "Be quiet!" She hoped there were no little animals in those piles of books— squirrels or chipmunks or even skunks—making Charlie bark. She headed back down the corridor. "What's up with Charlie?" her father asked as she zoomed into the kitchen.

"Hah!" Molly answered. "Good question! He's probably seen some animal in my room, scurrying around all that JUNK!"

"Calm down, Molly. What junk?"

"Those boxes and papers and things! That awful mess!"

"Oh, yeah! I'd forgotten all about that. It's just your grandpa Ernest's things." Dad handed her some frozen peas and nodded at the freezer. "Didn't Mom tell you? We had no room for it at the house, so we just had it shipped straight from England to the cottage."

"All of it?" Adam exclaimed. "But that house was full of stuff!" He remembered the house in Oxford from their many trips to England to see Gram. It had been like visiting a museum—a tacky old museum of ratty old furniture and worn carpets and cases full of dusty objects of all sorts, vases and sculptures and jewellery, and thousands and thousands of even dustier books and papers.

The place had given him the creepy crawlies. Even though he'd loved being with Gram, he had always been happy to come home again. In fact, Gram's house had pretty much convinced Adam that ghosts existed. One look at all that old stuff and you just knew the place was haunted—full of dark, mysterious forces just itching to get their hands on juicy young Barnetts to taunt them and tease them and torment them in ways ingenious and unimaginable. Just like in those Stephen King books he'd stolen from Molly's room and read when she wasn't looking.

And there was that thing that had happened the last time they were there, after Gram died. As they stood amidst the stacks of books and papers in his grandpa's old study, Adam's dad had gone very, very pale.

"What is it, Tim?" Mom had asked anxiously. "Are you all right?" She was already worried about his heart, even back then. Dad said no, no, he was fine. He said he'd just let his imagination carry him away, but he could have sworn he'd actually seen a ghost gazing at him—a scary looking ghoul with blazing eyes and weird, long, bright-red hair who turned out not to be there at all after Dad blinked and looked again.

Adam wasn't so convinced it was just imagination. After Dad told them what he thought he'd seen, Adam had gazed carefully at the desk himself—and for a moment, a horrible brief moment, he thought he'd actually seen someone there. Someone or something.

Something with red hair almost as awful as his own.

Adam shuddered as he slapped uselessly at the three or four mosquitoes buzzing around his head. He was glad the old place in Oxford had been sold and he'd never have to visit it again.

But all those things were here, right now, in the cottage at Falcon Lake. Even worse, they were in the room Molly never let anyone touch and always insisted on sleeping in. Well, let her sleep in it if she wanted to—he wasn't going anywhere near that stuff!

"We didn't bring all of it," Dad was saying as Molly continued to glare at him, her hands on her hips. "We sold a lot, and we just shipped over what your mom and I thought we might want to keep—my father's desk, his books, his papers. Your mom and I are planning to go through it while we're here at the lake. It's one of the reasons we decided to take the whole two weeks."

Molly shook her head in disbelief. Were her parents totally deranged? Why send all that stuff the entire way from England to the city and then pay more to have it shipped to Falcon Lake? Why not put it in the basement at home?

Thinking about it, though, Molly could sort of see the logic. It was bound to have been Mom's idea— just about everything that happened in their family was Mom's idea. But sending the stuff out here was a clever way of getting Dad out to the lake where they'd have to be together. At the cottage, Mom could keep an eye on him before his birthday and on his birthday and for a couple of weeks after his birthday, just to be on the safe side. If it wasn't for the boxes, he probably would have refused to come.

Molly sighed.

"Still," she grumbled, "I don't see why it has to be in my room." She hated the mess almost as much as she hated thinking about why they had to keep an eye on Dad.

"Molly, sweetie," said Dad, "come on. You know it's not *your* room. When we're not here, your cousins sleep in it. There are too many different people using this cottage for any one person to claim a room all for themselves."

"I know that," Molly said. "But I always stay there—except when Gram was here. And she isn't here now." For some reason, Molly didn't want to say the words "she's dead." She didn't want to make any reference to death. But Gram *was* dead, which was why the place in Oxford had been sold.

"Molly," said Dad, "quit obsessing and go out to the car and grab some groceries."

"But—"

Dad gave her an angry look. "Now, Molly."

He was so annoying. Cursing under her breath, she headed out to the car.

CHAPTER THREE
Ghost Calling

*T*he red-haired man sat at his desk wondering what had just happened.

The door had burst open and suddenly, a girl stood before him. A girl of about twelve, perhaps, with blue eyes, high cheekbones, a high forehead, and strawberry blond hair tied up in some rather odd formation on her head. She had stood there, suddenly silent, looking bewildered as she stared directly at him.

"Dad?" she'd said, her voice quivering.

"Molly!" A male voice had shouted from behind her. "Get in here this instant. . . ." And then, all at once, she was gone.

"Leeches! Eeeagh!"

This time, the voice came from outside the window. It was a child's voice, but not the girl. This was a boy, a clearly panic-stricken boy. The man rose from the desk and headed toward the window to see if he could find out what *was happening to the poor lad and, perhaps, come to his assistance.*

He fainted almost immediately.

"I hate leeches," muttered Adam to himself. "I hate them hate them hate them." He clung desperately to his green blow-up alligator, gazing through the crystal-clear water at what he considered to be the most disgusting, slimy creature alive. It lurked below, just waiting, Adam thought, for an unsuspecting toe to rest long enough so it could attach and blow itself up with his blood. And if there was one, Adam was sure there were probably thousands, millions even, the water in-fested with leeches, completely infested; just as the air was thick with mosquitoes. Hah! Mosquitoes! As if it wasn't bad enough that their bites itched all night so that he couldn't sleep, now there was the West Nile virus to worry about. He could end up with a fever, which would develop into a coma, and he'd be brain-damaged, and have to lie in bed, dreaming of swimming in the lake that had caused all his problems in the first place. He was, he realized, suspended between two hostile elements—in fact, the entire ecosystem seemed determined to feast on his blood one way or another.

Thank goodness for old Algie, he thought, patting the plastic alligator with his hand. Maybe he was too old for the alligator, like Molly was constantly telling him. But there was no-one around to see—no-one but Molly, and she didn't count.

Just then a horsefly dive-bombed his head. Great. On the bright side, though, at least these horrible creatures weren't out for his blood. They just wanted huge chunks of his flesh. Why had he let Molly talk him into going for a swim?

Adam tried to swat at the horsefly without tipping himself off of Algie. Still, even with the attack of the killer bugs, swimming was marginally better than having to put up with Dad while he put away all the groceries. What was it about putting groceries away that turned Dad into a total maniac?

It's because of the plan, Adam thought. His stupid grocery map.

Dad had a plan for everything. He'd sit down and spend hours figuring out the best, most logical, most efficient way of organizing things—and then he drew it up on a map, and issued copies, and made everyone stick to it. In the garage, the hose had to be near the garden tools but not too far from the car washing supplies—conveniently available for all the tasks it was used for. In the kitchen, the canned tomatoes had to be near both the basil and oregano and the taco supplies, within striking distance of the food processor, but not too far from the stove-top. The map for the kitchen at the lake was completely different from the one for the kitchen at home—to account for the different layout, of course, Dad said—and everyone in the family had a copy of each. They were to memorize the plans and use them at all times. In the Barnett family, you could be grounded for a week for putting the salt where the sugar was supposed to be.

But if he was being honest, Adam had to admit that he did kind of like it. He'd hate to put salt on his cereal just because it was in the wrong place in the cupboard. And all those maps and plans did make Dad a good producer. His television shows always ran like clockwork. "You can never be too logical," Dad always said. "Reason rules."

Perhaps it did. But you had to leave some room for imagination, didn't you? Because if you don't, Adam told himself as he kept swatting at the world's largest horsefly, I'm sunk.

And being rational did keep Dad busy. Adam certainly didn't have to worry about leaving him out of sight inside the cottage while he himself experienced torture outside in the water. Even far from the shore he could clearly hear his father cursing away about how he'd known there were already three bottles of spaghetti sauce out here (and where was he going to cram in three more without overcrowding the sauces section!) and who left the lid off the sugar (there were bound to be ants in it), and where were those nectarines (surely some thoughtless person hadn't managed to forget them because they'd certainly rot and stink up the kitchen before they got home), and so on and so on. He sounded upset enough to have a heart attack any minute.

Which was a good thing, Adam thought. As long as Dad was enjoying himself sounding hysterical and trying to make the world as rational as he thought it should be, he couldn't possibly have a heart attack. It was when things stopped being rational that they'd have to start worrying.

And they were at the lake. It was calm. It was normal. Nothing irrational ever happened here.

Except stupid irrational horseflies who dive-bombed the heads of perfectly innocent victims.

"Stupid horsefly!" he shrieked, flailing at it. "Go away!" It dived at him again and he knew he would soon have to make a choice, leap into the water to get away from it or be bitten.

Far out in the bay, Molly calmly watched Adam thrashing about on his stupid alligator and shouting. Probably fending off imaginary Viking warriors or something. Or battling the all too real bugs and leeches. She herself felt much calmer. As soon as she'd jumped into the water, she had stopped being upset. There was no point in being mad about the room, really—not when you could just jump into the blissfully cool lake and glide gently through the water, feeling it smooth against your skin, feeling the sun on your face. It felt like you'd just arrived in paradise. If you looked away from the cottage you could see the island situated just off the bay, and beyond it the long lake. If you looked towards land you saw the five cottages surrounded by white birch and fir trees. Those dark clouds that had swooped down on them as they drove were gone. The sky was a pure blue. And outside of Adam's shrieking it was completely quiet.

Molly had never understood Adam's fear of non-human creatures. Sure, occasionally a leech would get on her, but a bit of salt and it would drop right off. And the horseflies and mosquitoes were annoying, but no more than that. They wouldn't kill you, after all— unless you caught West Nile from them, and that surely wasn't very likely. But Adam acted as if the bugs were life-threatening all the time. To Molly they were the small price you paid for heaven.

She could feel the sun beating down on her bare head, and flipped backwards so it hit her full in the face. Her mind drifted back to the mess in her room. She'd figure out a way to get things back to exactly the way they should be before the day was out. There was no way the Wonder Woman room was going to be a mess. That would be even worse than dropping her favourite notebook in a mud puddle and having it end up with permanent black stains— an incident that had happened to her last spring. She still had nightmares.

As well as sorting out the room, she knew she'd have to keep an eye on Dad. He'd be at loose ends after he finished beating the kitchen into submission, and in need of lots of supervision. But Mom would soon head off the trouble at the hospital, just like she always did, and come out and take over from Molly. And then Molly would be free to lie for hours on the dock, like always, and she'd tell Adam to stop whining, like always, and the two of them would play countless games of Monopoly with the McDermots, like always. And Dad would be fine and the vacation would be as terrific as she'd always hoped and known it would be. It was just a matter of time.

"Molly!" At the sound of her name, Molly turned her head and looked toward the cottage. Her father was shouting as he ran onto the dock and he seemed to be upset about something. Upset at her. But she hadn't done anything to upset him, had she? She couldn't think of anything.

The last thing she wanted was for him to be upset. She waved at him to show she'd heard him and started to swim back in. But he was still running. He was always yelling at her and Adam for running on the dock, reminding them of how dangerous it was and that you could slip. But that didn't seem to be stopping him now.

"Molly! I'm coming!" he screamed. "Hold on!"

Charlie was bounding down the steps, too, trying

to catch up to Dad. The dog hit the deck and started to skid. For a moment Molly thought he would slide right into her dad, but instead he went sideways and ended up splashing into the lake.

Molly swam faster. Something was wrong—very wrong.

Suddenly, right in front of her dad, a large object appeared in a blinding flash of light. Standing in the middle of the dock was a woman in a long skirt. And all around the bright light was darkness. Darkness so black it was like a black hole.

But her dad didn't seem to see it. He just kept on running.

"Dad," she screamed, "watch out!"

If he heard her, it didn't seem to slow him down. He ran right into the darkness and the light.

And then, suddenly, her dad wasn't there. The woman wasn't there either, or the darkness, or the bright, white light.

Where was he? Where had he gone?

And then Molly saw. Her father was there—flat on his back on the dock!

Flat on his back, with nothing but the sunlight gleaming on him.

CHAPTER FOUR
The Chance of a Ghost

Molly swam as fast as she could, her heart pounding. Let him be okay, she prayed as she swam, let him be okay.

Adam was already out of the water when she reached the dock, hovering anxiously over Dad and dripping water on him.

"Now look what you've done!" he shouted at her. What was he talking about?

She pulled herself out of the water, heart in her throat. Was this how it would happen? Some freak accident? Was he? Could he . . . be dead?

But no, her dad was very much alive. He was holding onto his ankle and words were pouring out of his mouth that neither Molly nor Adam had heard before.

"Is it broken?" she asked.

35

Dad stopped swearing long enough to take a closer look. No bones were sticking out, but a nasty bruise was already beginning to form.

"I'm pretty sure it's just a nasty twist," he said, then turned and gave her a grim look. "No thanks to you, Molly." Before Molly could reply, Charlie scrambled out of the water. He leaped onto the deck, bounded over to Tim, and nudged his leg with his nose. "Ouch, Charlie, no!" Dad scolded.

"No thanks to me?" Molly said, ignoring Charlie. What was Dad talking about?

"Yes, to you, Molly! Why were you shouting like that?"

"Shouting? But——"

"You really scared me! I thought you were drowning."

"But I wasn't shouting! I wasn't saying anything! I was just floating."

"Oh, come on, Molly," said Adam. "You were so shouting. You were calling to Dad, telling him he had to come. You scared me, too. And now look what you've done! You've broken his leg."

"It's not broken," Dad said. "It's just a nasty twist." He reached down to touch it again and winced.

"See!" exclaimed Adam. "It could be broken even if it doesn't look broken."

"I wasn't shouting," Molly shouted. "I wasn't!" Had they both gone crazy?

36

Adam was too upset to listen. "We need to go back to the city right away. Dad needs a doctor."

"I did not shout," Molly insisted. "I swear I didn't shout."

But she *had* shouted, Adam thought. And then Dad had run out onto the dock, and then—the light! There was a weird light on the dock. And Dad sort of, well, ran into it. Just before he fell.

Adam opened his mouth to tell the others about the light—and then closed it again.

If he told Molly, she'd say it was only his imagination. Just once, he thought, just once he wished she would be the one to notice weird things.

"Dad," said Molly, tears in her eyes, "I didn't shout, I didn't. You have to believe me!"

"Woohoo! Everything all right over there?"

Who was that? Adam looked around. There was someone standing on the Rosen's dock, a man in a shirt with great big pink and orange flowers on it. Lots of flowers, because the shirt was huge, huge enough to fit the man, who was practically a giant. As all of them watched, he ran to the shore and then rushed along the small path in the bush between cottages, the bright flowers on his shirt catching the sun as he moved through the trees and leaped up onto the dock. It seemed like just a second ago that he'd been on the Rosen's dock, and now he was crouching down to take a close look at Dad's ankle. "Hmm," he said. "Not good. Not good at all."

"But . . . but . . . ," Dad sputtered, then added, "ouch," as the man carefully poked his ankle with one of his large fingers.

"Who are you?" Molly asked, forgetting all her manners.

"Yes, who?" said Dad, wincing once more as the finger hit another tender spot.

"Reggie," he said. "Reggie Crankshaft, registered nurse. Staying at the Rosen's cottage. Rented it for two weeks. Needed a vacation. Stand back."

Before Molly even realized what was happening, Reggie had picked Dad up as if he weighed nothing, carried him up the stairs to the cottage, put him on the couch, found a footstool, and put his foot up on it.

"There," the nurse said, wiping his hands on the pink and orange flowers that covered his massive chest. "That will do nicely. Now it needs some ice." He turned to Molly and Adam, who were hovering behind him trying, unsuccessfully, to see how Dad was taking it all.

"We don't have any ice," Molly interrupted. "We just got here and the trays we put in the fridge won't be frozen yet."

"I have some. I'll be right back," said Reggie. And as quick as he had appeared he was gone.

"Maybe Adam is right, Dad," Molly said. "We should go back to the city and you should see a doctor."

"And will you be driving?"

Molly was shocked. It wasn't like Dad to be sarcastic. Angry, yes. Strict, yes. Sarcastic, no.

Dad glared at her as he spoke, obviously still blaming her for his fall. This had gone on long enough already, and she was beginning to get frightened. Had she lost her mind or had her dad and her brother lost theirs? They both swore she had screamed for help. She knew she hadn't.

And what had she seen just before her dad fell? Something very, very strange. Should she mention it? Well, they already blamed her. What did she have to lose?

"Dad," she said, pushing Charlie's wet head away. He'd just padded into the room, still soaking wet. "Honestly, I did not shout. And I saw something."

Adam looked at her sharply. She'd seen something, too?

But before she could say anything more Reggie was back with the ice.

"Here," Reggie said.

Charlie took one look at the giant nurse and slunk under the table in the corner. Why, wondered Adam, wasn't he jumping or barking the way he usually did when strangers came into the house? It was a good thing he wasn't, though. If he started acting normal now, there'd be water flying all over the place.

Adam stared at Reggie and wondered how anyone could make it between those two cottages that fast! It was as if he had appeared by magic, like Tinkerbell in *Peter Pan*, except without the fairy dust.

And Reggie sure wasn't any Tinkerbell. He was at least six foot four, with short, jet black hair, shoulders like a linebacker, and a square jaw that declared how tough he was. He looked like he could take on anyone, anywhere.

And yet he was being very gentle with Dad.

"There," Reggie said, carefully placing the ice around Dad's ankle, "that will do it."

"Should we take him to the hospital?" Molly asked anxiously. "Will he be okay?"

"I can tell you that it's certainly not a break," Reggie said, bending down and examining the ankle closely once more. "Bad sprain, though. No, the hospital isn't necessary—but he'll need to stay off it for a couple days."

He turned and looked at Molly and Adam. The way he curled his lips suggested he didn't much like what he was seeing. "It just goes to show you what happens when you pretend you're in trouble," he said, looking right at Molly. "Good heavens, young lady, don't the schools teach water safety any more?"

"But I didn't—"

Molly stopped, silenced by the look of pure disbelief on Reggie's face. He had heard it, too? What was the matter with everyone?

"Well, one thing's for sure," Reggie continued. "You children are going to need looking after."

Children! Really! He is infuriating, thought Molly. "Is there a mother involved here at all?" Reggie added.

Dad assured the nurse that there was and she'd be out, hopefully by dinner time.

"Good," Reggie said. "I'm happy to help until then. I'll just go lock up the Rosen's and be back here in a jiff." He turned to leave the room.

"We couldn't ask you to do that, Mr., uh, Mr. Crankshaft, is it?"

"Just call me Reggie," the nurse said, "and don't worry about it. I'm happy to help. I was getting bored sitting out there on that dock all the time. Need something to do."

"But Mr. Crankshaft—"

"Reggie. Call me Reggie." It sounded like an order.

"Uh, Reggie."

"That's right. Reggie. And you are . . . ?"

"Tim, Tim Barnett."

"Pleased to meet you, Tim." He grabbed Tim's hand and pumped it up and down vigorously, lifting Tim almost off the sofa with each pump. "And

41

these, uh, these . . . ?" Reggie pointed toward Molly and Adam.

"That's Molly, and that's Adam. And we're quite capable of—"

"I see."

Molly began to stick out her hand, assuming the nurse would want to shake it. But he simply gave her and Adam a dark look and turned back to their father.

"There's no point trying to stop me, Tim," he said. "I won't take no for an answer. I never do."

I believe it, thought Molly. Who would have the guts to say no to him?

"These youngsters need to be taken in hand," Reggie continued, "and you can't do it. No, Tim, you just sit there and keep your foot up on that stool. I'll be back in a snap to see about getting you all some lunch."

And once more, he was gone.

As soon as Reggie left the room, Charlie came out from under the table in the corner. Whining, he made his way over to Adam and licked his hand.

Adam gave the dog a reassuring pat on the head and reminded himself to try to dry him off a little. Why was Charlie acting so strangely? Now that Reggie was gone Charlie seemed so—well, so relieved.

Just like Adam.

There was something strange about that nurse, he mused. Something very strange. Reggie was too big, too fast—too everything. Being with him was like being rolled over by a king-sized lawn roller. Except creepier. It was like being rolled over by a king-sized lawn roller with horror-movie music playing in the background and green blood oozing out of the grass.

And the king-sized lawn roller had said he'd be back soon. What had Molly and her stupid shouting got them into?

There was another voice out there now—a strangely familiar voice saying, or rather shouting, "Just call me Reggie." It was a loud, deep voice. Where had he heard it before? Not so long ago, it was—and he had some very bad feelings about it. What had happened? Why couldn't he remember?

And furthermore, why couldn't he go and see who it was, see what the man looked like? Why couldn't he leave the desk without fainting? Now he could hear other voices, too. One of them was that girl he'd seen before, shouting something about not shouting. He wished she would return so that he could warn her about that other voice.

But warn her in what way? Say what? What did he need to warn her against, exactly? Why couldn't he remember?

Damnation!

He threw his pen down in disgust. He needed to figure out what was happening, and soon, before he went quite mad!

CHAPTER FIVE
The Vanishing Ghost

Molly was doing her best to listen to Dad talk to Mom on the phone, but it was hard to concentrate. Reggie was issuing order after order and giving Molly black look after black look as she failed, again and again, to move quickly enough or to do things exactly the way Reggie expected.

"No, no, not there," he said as Molly put the mustard down in front of him. "Here!" He moved the mustard bottle about a quarter of an inch to the left. "That's much better."

It was like being in grade one again, she grumbled to herself, except with a prison guard as your teacher—a very scary prison guard in a ghastly pink and orange shirt, and with a large knife in his very large hand. And a look on his face that suggested he wouldn't hesitate to use it if Molly didn't cooperate.

45

It wouldn't have been half as annoying if what he wanted wasn't so wrong. Molly had put the mustard bottle down exactly in the very best place for it to be, if you wanted to make sandwiches as efficiently as possible. She had made sandwiches herself many times, and she had figured out exactly the best place for each of the condiments—including the mustard, which needed to be a few inches to the right of the margarine and just to the left of the hot peppers. But Reggie made her move it. Really! Who did he think he was anyway?

Still, even if Reggie wasn't as well organized as he ought to be, Molly had to admit that he was whipping up an amazing meal—mile-high deli sandwiches, pickles, hot peppers, and chips. He had the chips on the wrong side of the sandwiches, but Molly could fix that on her own plate later. And for all the close calls Molly's fingers had had with that knife he was wielding, they were still attached to her hands.

Maybe, Molly told herself as she looked at the sandwiches, her mouth watering, maybe he's not so bad after all. Maybe I'm just imagining it.

Reggie had certainly managed to get Dad comfortable. And once Dad finally gave in and agreed to let Reggie stay and help, his mood improved. He actually seemed to be quite happy. Make that very happy. Right now, he was lying on the couch with his foot propped up on pillows, a glass of ice water and a stack of magazines close at hand, as he tried to explain the situation to Mom.

The kitchen Molly stood in was really just one end of the living room, so she should have been able to hear every word Dad was saying—and maybe even some of Mom's responses. But Reggie wouldn't stop issuing orders.

"Those milk glasses are too full," said Reggie. "They'll spill for sure."

"He's a registered nurse," said Dad. "He's staying at the Rosen's."

"Here," said Reggie, grabbing the jug of milk out of Molly's hands. "Let me."

"There's no need for you to come out," Dad said. "None at all. Reggie . . . yeah, that's right, his name is Reggie. He and Molly are in the kitchen right now, making lunch." He looked up at Reggie and smiled. Reggie gave him a huge smile back, revealing an even row of white, gleaming teeth. "Molly? Sure." He turned to Molly. "She wants to talk to you."

Molly sighed, and went over to the phone. The moment of truth.

She needed to make Mom believe that she hadn't shouted. But why should Mom believe her when Dad wouldn't? Sure, it wasn't the kind of childish thing Molly ever did. She was way too mature for that, and Mom knew it. Everyone always joked that she'd been born way too mature! But this was no joke. Still, everyone else insisted it had happened. She hadn't screamed! She knew she hadn't. Was she going crazy?

"Hi, Mom."

"Molly! How on earth did this happen? Why were you shouting when nothing was wrong?"

"Mom, I wasn't, I promise you! You know I'd never do a thing like that."

"Which is why it's so disappointing! And *especially* now, of *all* times."

"But, Mom, really, you have to believe me, I—"

"We're not going to discuss this right now. We're just not." Molly could tell from the deep breath her mother took that she was trying to stay calm. "What I would like to know," Mom continued, "is why you were out on the lake at all. Why weren't you with him, Molly?"

Now Molly felt really guilty. She should have helped her dad with the unpacking. She shouldn't have left his side. She'd made a promise to her mom, and now she'd broken it.

"Sorry," she said meekly.

"I really think you should all come home," Mom said. "Dad's had one accident, already—one that might easily have been avoided."

Does she have to rub it in? thought Molly.

"And this makes him more prone to . . . well . . . to something else if anything more happens to him.

Every little bit of excitement only makes it worse. And what if one of *you* needs help, what if one of you slips? What will happen then?"

"Well," Molly said, keeping her voice as low as possible, "we do have a nurse." She did her best to sound cheerful about it. It would be a complete disaster if Mom found out how she really felt about Reggie. But she couldn't stop herself from adding, in a whisper she hoped Reggie wouldn't hear, "A huge nurse."

"Huge?" Mom asked.

"Really, Mom, huge!" Maybe Mom would think a larger one would offer even more good care.

Mom laughed. Molly let out a breath. Whew. Mom could still laugh!

"And you think this huge nurse can handle Dad?"

Handle him? He could beat him in a wrestling match with one arm tied behind his back. He could stare him into surrender with one glance from his black eyes.

"Yes, Mom," Molly said. "He seems very capable."

"OK, I guess. Let me talk to Dad."

Molly handed the phone back, her fingers crossed.

Dad listened for a few moments, then said goodbye and clicked off, grinning like a little boy who had just gotten away with whatever little boys try to get away with.

"We're staying."

49

"Excellent," Reggie declared as he carried in a tray of sandwiches.

"Adam!" Molly shouted. "Lunch!"

Where had he gone?

Adam had decided to put his bag in his room. He thought it would be a good excuse to get away from the nurse, who was making Adam even more nervous than usual as he waved around that big, sharp knife. Besides which, Adam was a little miffed. Reggie had ordered Molly to help him with lunch and hadn't even bothered to say no when Adam offered to help. Adam hated being ignored.

Adam's room was right beside Molly's—the first one just off the corridor leading from the living room. He'd unpacked and then tried to block out the phone call he knew was coming. There was no way he wanted to hear his mom's reaction to this accident. No such luck. The cottage was too small, and as he sat on his bed trying to read a comic he could hear Dad talking and imagine what Mom was saying back. "You did what? And where was Molly when it happened? Where was Adam?"

It was clear she wasn't happy and Adam didn't want to hear another word. He decided to go read his comic in Molly's room down the hall. All that junk was there, of course, and just the thought of that old house and the dusty, weird stuff in it creeped him out. But listening to Dad talk to Mom was worse. He hurried down the hall and opened the door. There were only about a dozen boxes, stacked up in front of an old desk, and they didn't look the least bit dusty. What was Molly so upset about anyway? How could she let a few boxes bother her so much? Especially when there were more important things to worry about. Like Dad. Dad and the family curse. Adam's grandfather had died just before his thirty-fifth birthday—and that was his desk, wasn't it? Hoping the boxes wouldn't suddenly decide to topple and crush him to death, Adam stepped in between two large stacks so he could get a clearer view of the desk.

And there was Dad, sitting behind the desk and staring at Adam as if he were seeing a ghost. Adam almost wanted to rub his eyes. How had Dad grown his hair so long in the few moments since he'd just seen him? Or was he wearing a wig?

"No, no. Don't worry about it!" It was a voice from the living room. Dad's voice, still talking to Mom on the phone.

But how could he talk on the phone in the living room and be here behind the desk at the same time?

"Tim?" said the dad behind the desk.

"Dad?" It did sound exactly like him.

A sudden smile brightened the man's face. "I know!" he said, wonder in his voice. "I *wondered* why you looked so familiar. It's because you look exactly like my son Tim. Except a few years older. He's just five now—and you must be two or three years older than that."

Adam was insulted. "I'm ten," he said, with ice in his voice. "Almost eleven."

"Ten? Really? I'd never have. . . . Well, anyway, you look exactly the way Tim will probably look in a few years. How very peculiar."

"You think that's strange?" said Adam. "You look just like my dad does right now, except for the long hair. He's out there in the other room—that's his voice you can hear—and his name is Tim!"

They both stared at each other for a moment and neither spoke.

Adam was wondering if he should scream. It seemed exactly like the kind of situation which called for a scream. But somehow, he didn't actually feel like screaming. He wasn't even particularly frightened. Well, that scraggly long hair was pretty scary, but it's hard to get too alarmed just looking at what was more or less your own familiar father.

Maybe I've finally gone crazy, he thought.

Or. . . . Suddenly, Adam was very excited. Maybe it's because it's really happening this time! Maybe the aliens have finally landed! Wouldn't that be something! To finally have one of the bizarre things he was always imagining come true!

If he could get this sort-of-Dad creature to come out to the living room with him, they'd all see him. See him and Dad together in the same room! Then everyone would have to believe him! Even Molly would have to stop teasing him about his imagination.

"Adam! Lunch!"

Lunch! The perfect way to get the sort-of-Dad into the living room!

"You're not hungry, are you, Sir? It's just sandwiches, but I'm sure there'd be enough for one more."

"Come to think of it," the sort-of-Dad said, "I am rather hungry. For some time now I've been smelling the most delicious odour of salted beef."

Salted beef? "It's pastrami, I think," said Adam.

"Whatever it is, it does smell wonderful. I believe I will join you." The man stood up and began to come around the desk.

And then he disappeared. Suddenly vanished into thin air.

This time, Adam did scream—but he was so frightened that the scream came out as more of a squeaky gasp than a real scream. He turned, charged back in between the boxes, bolted out of the room, and somehow made it to the living room without noticing his feet touching the ground.

After grabbing a sandwich from the tray on the coffee table, he sat down beside Molly at the table and started to stuff it into his mouth. Maybe he was just faint from hunger, he thought, and his imagination had run away with him. Again. As usual.

Adam was so upset he just sat there and ate, not saying a single word.

CHAPTER SIX
Ghostly Meeting

With a sandwich in one hand, and a potato chip in the other, Molly was munching. Munching and thinking.

There had to be a way to get them to believe her, she thought. Otherwise the whole shout thing was going to drive her totally insane. She hadn't shouted. She knew for sure she hadn't. But she had seen something—something no one else seemed to have seen. It was a light, a strange light. She'd seen Dad come out onto the dock shouting for her and he'd run right into it. And then he fell. And then, suddenly, the light wasn't there anymore. What could account for it?

Because it *had* to be accounted for. Molly knew there was a rational explanation for it. There was a rational explanation for everything. This wasn't Adam's world, after all. This was her world—the real world!

The light was probably just an illusion, she thought—the sun shining on a puddle of water on the dock. And maybe Reggie was a ventriloquist. After all, he'd shown up just when the accident happened. Maybe he'd been standing there on the Rosen's dock the whole time. Maybe he was the one who had been shouting.

But his voice was way too deep. He sounded like a bullfrog—Dad and Adam would never confuse that with her voice.

Unless he disguised it.

But why would he? Why would he want to pretend to be Molly? He was a nurse, just an ordinary guy renting a cottage at the lake. A large, strange, scary, ordinary guy—but still. Just because she didn't like him didn't mean he was bad. Did it?

"Excellent sandwich, Reggie," said Dad. "But I'd like just a little more mustard." He swung his feet off the couch and onto the floor, ready to head for the kitchen.

"Oh, no you don't," said Reggie.

Reggie had been sitting at the table gulping down whole sandwiches as if each one was a breath mint, but in an instant he was by the sofa, staring down at Dad. "You just stay off that foot, Mister."

Dad sank back down on to the sofa.

"Yes, Sir," he said.

Molly stared at her dad. Was he joking? He never

talked to anyone like that—so . . . so . . . meekly. Had Reggie put a spell on him or something? Molly almost snorted, laughing at herself. Now she really was starting to think like Adam!

"That's better," said Reggie. "I'll get the mustard." And Dad had the mustard in his hand before Molly could blink her eyes.

"Uh, thanks," said Dad, with a smile.

"No problem," said Reggie. "You just leave everything to me."

Everything? thought Molly. What did everything mean?

Adam interrupted her thoughts. "Molly," he said quietly, "what do you think?"

"About what?"

"Can someone be in two places at the same time?"

Adam had to ask her, because the more he thought about it, the more real it seemed. It wasn't like imagining something at all. It felt, well, real. Really real.

And so what if he—it . . . whatever—just blinked out like that? That didn't mean it wasn't real, right? Fireflies were real, and they blinked out all the time.

Of course, he had to admit he'd never seen a person do it before. Thank heavens. But still. . . .

"Two places at once?" said Molly. "You mean like in a sci-fi movie?"

"Yeah . . . like that."

"Impossible."

There he goes again, she thought. Why did she have to end up with Mr. Weirdthought Mindscramble for a brother? Then, suddenly, she stopped and stared at him. Two people in the same place. Earlier, in the bedroom. Behind the desk. Dad—it *was* Dad— but Dad had also been out in the kitchen, putting away groceries!

"Why?" she asked Adam, turning her head sharply and looking at him. "Have you seen something?"

"No! No! My mind was probably just wandering. I mean, Dad was here on the couch, right? There's no way he could have been in your room behind a desk. Right?"

Molly almost choked on her hot peppers. Dad? Behind the desk? Adam saw him, too? She took a large swig of milk and stood up.

"Adam is going to help me sort those boxes," she announced.

No way. Adam shook his head. He was *not* going back in there. Not with Molly acting so strangely. She couldn't possibly think it was real—could she?

Because if Molly thought it was real, Adam told himself, then it *was* real. He could feel the scream beginning to form in the pit of his stomach.

But before it could begin to climb up his gut and arrive at his mouth, Molly grabbed his arm and practically lifted him out of his chair. She dragged him out of the living room and down the hall.

"I'm not going back in there," Adam hissed, not wanting Dad to hear and get upset. "I'm not. I'm not."

"We're going in together," Molly said. "I'll be there to protect you. Don't be a wimp." And, she added to herself, Adam would be there to protect her. Even she had to admit it—she was getting just a little weirded out.

"There's a logical explanation," she said to Adam. "There always is. Maybe . . . well . . . hey, maybe there's a portrait that came with the desk, ever think of that? A painting of Dad, maybe?"

"No, I hadn't!" Adam said, feeling immensely relieved. Of course there was an explanation. There always was—and it was never any of the upsetting ones that he came up with. No aliens involved.

But . . . wait a minute! Had he been talking to a portrait? Paintings can't talk.

I must have lost my mind, Adam told himself. And I definitely do not want to go back to the place where I lost it. It might still be lying there on the floor, a mass of pulsating grey matter, calling me towards it. I might step on it by accident and stamp out some of my best thoughts.

"Come on," said Molly, still dragging him. Once in front of the closed door, though, she hesitated, a look of fear on her face.

59

It was about time she realized how scary this was, Adam thought. "Not quite so sure now, huh?" he said aloud.

Which was a mistake. Molly would never admit she was scared of anything. Or, for that matter, uncertain. "Of course I'm sure," she retorted, and she flung the door open and stepped over the threshold.

Adam's heart sank. He'd been hoping she was going to chicken out. Instead, she reached behind her, grabbed his arm and pulled him in, closing the door behind her.

"Hello?" she called. She couldn't see anything past the boxes, but she wasn't willing to go nearer to the desk.

"Hello?" A voice came back, rather faint, but definitely there.

Molly grabbed Adam's hand and pulled him along as she slowly made her way forward, gingerly stepping past the boxes. She took a deep breath, and dragging Adam, finally stood right in front of the desk.

There he was. Dad. Dad with ridiculous long hair, looking extremely dishevelled, and staring at her and Adam as if they were ghosts.

"Good heavens!" he exclaimed, standing up, "Tim, my lad? Is it you again? You know I don't like you to come in here when I'm—"

And then, suddenly, the strangest look crossed

his face. "Tim—my boy, my son, my only son! You're not . . . you're not dead, are you?"

"Dead?" said Molly and Adam in unison.

"Of course not," added Molly.

Adam wasn't so sure. If you could be scared to death, like people always said, then he had to be at least halfway there.

In fact, he felt quite faint. He stepped back, sank onto the bed, and stared.

Molly walked up to the desk and stretched her arm out in front of her, trying to touch the man. Except her hand went right through him. Adam felt woozy, very woozy. He saw black and then nothing.

"Wake up! Wake up!" It was Molly, shaking him, shouting at him.

He looked around. He was lying on Molly's bed. There were boxes all around. He said, "I just had the weirdest dream. We were in your room, the Wonder Woman room, and. . . ."

"Shut up, Adam!" Molly ordered, too rattled to even pretend to be nice. "It isn't a dream. Unless I'm having the same one—which is impossible. Get up." She grabbed his shoulder and forced him onto his feet.

"Is he all right?" It was Dad talking—the dad behind the desk, the one with the long hair.

"Not," the man added, "that he could really be anything but all right. He *is* a spirit, after all." Although the man was gazing at Adam, he seemed to be talking to himself, as if he were trying to figure something out. "He has to be a spirit—it's the obvious explanation." He spoke to Adam. "Yes. You're Tim and yet not quite Tim. Tim, but looking a little older."

"But I'm not . . . ," Adam began. But the man was too busy thinking to hear him.

"According to McBrattle and Logan in *The Physiology of the Afterlife*," he said, "those fortunate ones who experience sightings often see the spirits of their dear departed ones looking different from the way they did at the moment of their decease. Some look younger, McBrattle and Logan say, and some much older—as if they revealed after life their truest selves, the essential being hidden within their mortal physical shell. And little Timmie always seems older than his years. Always looking for rational explanations, always insisting there's a logical reason for everything, poor deluded lad. I have no idea where he gets it—not from me, certainly. But . . . but if I see Tim, but older, then—" Suddenly he began to sob. "Oh, I can't bear it!" he said, between sobs, staring at Adam. "My Timmie, dead! You were so young, Timmie my lad, so very young. And—" his face changed—"and it's my fault! It must be! This is where my endless meddling with the spirit world has led me! The spirits have had their revenge!"

He reached across the desk to Adam, imploring. "Oh, my boy, I never intended it to be like this. How cruel fate can be. It finally shows me a spirit— and it is the ghost of my own son! My Tim! My darling little Timmie!"

"But . . . ," said Adam, bewildered, taking a step back.

"Look, Sir," Molly said impatiently. This had gone on quite long enough. "I don't know what you're upset about it, but I do know you don't have to be."

"I don't?" The man stopped sobbing and looked at her.

"Not about that, anyway. Because he's not dead. And he's not Tim. His name is Adam, and he's my brother."

"Your brother? Not my Timmie?"

"No, not your Timmie. But. . . ." Molly hesitated. It was all so strange, and somehow saying it would make it seem very real.

"Tim is my dad's name," Adam said, his voice quavering a bit, "like I told you before. My dad is Tim Barnett, and he's out there in the other room."

"Barnett, you said? Tim Barnett? Your *father* is Tim Barnett?"

Molly and Adam both nodded.

"It can't be."

"It is," said Molly. "And I'm Molly, and this is Adam. And," she added, gesturing around the room, "this is our cottage. What are you doing here? Who are you?"

"I'm Ernest Barnett," the man answered, sounding very bewildered.

"Ernest Barnett?" said Molly, incredulous. "You have the same last name as we do?"

"I think so. When I woke up this morning, I was Ernest Barnett. When I had my breakfast, I was Ernest Barnett. When I came into my study to get some work done, I was Ernest Barnett. But now . . . ," he looked around the room again, his face a little green. "Now I'm not sure. This is my desk, certainly, but. . . ." He looked around the room, bewildered and then sat down. "I don't feel well. Not well at all."

"Okay," said Molly, "now I'm *really* confused. Because Ernest Barnett—well, Ernest Barnett is our grandfather. This is his desk. And *he's* dead."

The man's eyes looked like they were going to pop right out of his head. "Your grandfather?" he said. "Dead? But I'm not—I can't be—" Suddenly he clutched at his chest.

"Are you all right?"

The man was gasping for breath, choking, his face turning bright red.

"We'd better call Dad," Molly said, and turned to run out of the room.

She'd almost made it to the door when she heard Adam speak.

"He's gone," he said, his voice surprisingly calm. "Again."

She turned back to see that it was true. The man was, indeed, gone. Literally gone. There was no one behind the desk.

"But—" Molly's mind couldn't grasp it. He'd looked as if he was dying. And then, well, he simply wasn't there anymore.

And then, all at once, he *was* there. Again. Not choking, not gasping for breath.

"Oh dear," he said, wiping his hand across his brow. "What happened?"

"I . . . I don't know," said Molly. She was beginning to freak out. She could have sworn the man was having a heart attack. Mom had made her and Adam go through the first-aid drill again and again. Molly knew all the signs, and the signs were all there. When Adam said he was gone, she was sure he meant the man had died.

But he hadn't—Adam had meant something quite different. Different, and much, much weirder.

And now, well, it was just like nothing at all had happened. The man behind the desk looked a little excited, but perfectly okay.

She wanted to run, to get away from it all, to find a place where things were normal, orderly, rational—the way they should be. But she couldn't. She felt glued to the spot, as if she were in one of those dreams where you're so scared you can't move, even though you want to.

With all this happening, she realized, Adam must be going out of his mind. She turned to comfort him—and saw that he didn't seem scared at all.

"I get it," he said, a strange smile on his face. "I think I understand what's happening."

CHAPTER SEVEN
A Family Ghost

"What are you talking about, Adam?" said Molly.

"He just died," said Adam. "He just died again."

"Died?" said the man.

"Again?" said Molly.

"Yes," said Adam. "Died. Again." Now that he thought about it, it was all so obvious.

"But I don't see—" said the man.

"Adam," said Molly imploringly. "Give. Now. What are you talking about?" And, she thought, why aren't you acting like yourself? Why aren't you shaking in your boots? She felt a sudden urge to start shouting for Dad—and held it in. That would be a particularly terrible mistake. If it alarmed *her*. . . .

"It's like this," said Adam. "This really is our granddad."

"He is?" said Molly.

"I am?" said the man.

"He is. You are. He has to be, Molly. It's the only thing that makes sense. He looks exactly like Dad—and remember, Gram always said Dad looks like his dad did."

Molly could remember it clearly. "The spitting image," Gram was always saying, "except for the hair, of course. I never could talk that silly man into getting a sensible haircut. Seemed to think that ridiculous mop would get the undergraduates on his side, make them think he was young like them. Never realized it was already out of fashion. Never realized how much it made them laugh at him, poor dear, even though they certainly respected him otherwise."

Gram was totally right about the hair.

"And," Adam went on, "he says his name is Ernest Barnett, and like you said, our granddad's name was Ernest Barnett. And he has a son named Tim, just like our granddad did, and he thought I was him—and I look like dad, right?"

"It's true," the man said, a thoughtful look on his face. "I am Ernest Barnett. And I am Tim's father—and you do look a lot like him. Hmmm."

"Yes, but. . . ." Molly wasn't convinced. There was something not quite right about it.

Ah yes, of course!

"But Adam," she said, "this can't be our granddad Ernest. Our granddad Ernest is dead."

The logic was incontrovertible. She smiled triumphantly.

"You needn't look so happy about it, dear," said the man.

Oops. "Sorry, Sir," she said. "But, really, it makes no sense. I mean, yes, you do look like our dad. You look exactly like him, except for that awful mop of—well, except for a few small differences. And that means you can't be our grandfather—because if you *were* our granddad and you were still alive you'd be really, really old and have grey hair and wrinkles and much, much less hair. And it hardly matters, anyway, because our granddad Ernest is dead."

"Well," he said, "I'm certainly not dead. Why, look at me! Do I look old? You've already mentioned my youthful hair! The undergraduates are always telling me how it is, as they like to say, 'groovy.'" Smiling, he ran his hand through it. "I'm in the prime of life. Oh, to be sure, I have been told by the doctors that I have a tricky heart, and I am to avoid sudden shocks. But otherwise, I'm fit as a fiddle. Still young. Still healthy."

"It's so simple," Adam said, delighted to finally be the one explaining things. "Think about it. How can he be our granddad and young and here and dead all at the same time? It's obvious."

"It is?"

"Of course! He's a ghost!"

"A ghost?"

"I'm a ghost?" the ghost said. "But I can't be. I'm not dead."

"Sorry, Sir," said Adam, "but I think you are. You died many years ago, back when our dad was just little. It was just before your thirty-fifth birthday, and—"

"My thirty-fifth birthday! That's right, it's tomorrow!"

"Except you never made it to your birthday."

The man looked completely bewildered. "But it can't be," he said. Then he gave Adam a questioning look. "Look here—how do I know that *you're* not the ghosts? How do I know you two aren't spirits sent to confuse me and keep me from my quest? How can you be so sure that I'm not alive and you're the ones who are dead?"

For a moment there was silence.

"Got you there, lad, eh?" said the man, smiling triumphantly.

And, thought Molly, he did have a point. It was all too bizarre, too unsettling. Nothing could make it more sensible—not even she and Adam being dead.

"I'm sorry, Sir," said Adam, "but I don't think so. We can leave this room. We can go into the living room, or out to the lake. And you—well, you can't. You can't leave that desk."

"Don't be silly, lad," the man said. "Of course I can. See, I'll just get up out of the chair and come around there, and you'll see that—"

As he spoke, he got out of the chair, stepped away from the desk—and faded.

Adam and Molly stood transfixed. Molly was too shocked to even think. And even though he'd been expecting it to happen and wasn't the least bit surprised, Adam still found it unsettling. The man—Granddad—seemed so completely real. And then he wasn't. Wasn't anything.

And then he was. Because now he was back again, still standing, leaning on the edge of the desk. It was worse than watching a magician make balls appear and disappear under cups.

"I did it again," he said, sheepishly. "I did it before, and I couldn't understand it. And now, I just did it again. Didn't I?"

"Yes," said Adam. "You did."

"Then," he said, "you must be right. I must be a ghost. I must be . . . dead." He went back behind the desk and dropped into the chair. He looked devastated, crushed.

"I told you," said Adam, turning to Molly with a triumphant smile. "It's the only rational explanation."

Rational, thought Molly! This is rational? If this is rational, then I'm a fat green whistling teakettle. And yet, it did seem like the only possible explanation.

Darn. I might as well just start boiling and whistling and turning green right now, she thought, grimly.

"I am dead," Granddad said. "I really am dead. I am thirty-five. Except it seems I have been dead for many years, without being aware of it. I've been sitting at my desk, working as usual, and have not realized any time has passed. I did wonder about the scenery outside my window changing. That certainly gave me pause. But nevertheless, I was just thinking Dora would soon call me for dinner."

The look on his face changed. "Oh, dear," he said. "Dora. I hope she didn't take it too hard, poor dear." He looked up at Molly. "Did she?"

Molly didn't know what to say. If she told him her grandma had been broken-hearted by his sudden death, which was true, he'd feel bad for her. But if she told him Grandma had simply taken it in stride and got on with the rest of her life as a widow with a small son, as, eventually, she also did, he'd feel bad for himself.

"It was so long ago," she finally said. "Years and years before I was born. I don't really know how Gram felt about it way back then. But I do know she always loved you. She was always talking about you."

"Always," agreed Adam. After listening to Gram go on and on about her wonderful Ernest whenever they saw her, Adam figured he knew almost as much about the red-haired man sitting in front of him as he did about himself. "Did you really eat your broccoli with chocolate sauce?"

"I did," Granddad said, nodding. "A very healthy combination. And tasty. You should try it."

"No way," Adam said. The mere thought of it made his stomach turn.

"She told you about that, eh?" Granddad said. "Poor dear. She must have been so lonely."

"I don't think she was too lonely," Molly said. "Oh, she missed you, of course. She missed you a lot. And she never got married again."

"Never remarried! You don't say!"

"Never," Molly said. She decided she wouldn't mention Gram's good friend Derrick, who had always been a kind of substitute granddad for her and Adam, and who was still over in England taking Gram's death much harder than Granddad seemed to be taking his own.

"Of course," Adam said, "she always had Dad—at least until he met Mom at college and decided to come back here with her. And Gram came here to visit us each year, and we went to Oxford to visit her whenever we could."

A look of perplexity suddenly crossed Granddad's face. "Came? Went? You don't do it anymore?"

Oh dear, thought Molly. This is going to be bad.

"We can't," she said. "Gram is. . . . Well, Gram died last year."

"Dora dead?" Granddad shook his head. "My dear, darling Dora, gone?" Suddenly, he started to weep. "Oh, Dora, Dora," he gasped, choking between breaths. "My lovely Dora! My——" Now he was gasping for breath, choking, unable to speak!

Oh no! thought Molly. He's doing it again. And it's really bad this time.

She ran behind the desk, trying not to panic, trying to remember what you were supposed to do during a heart attack. She put her arm over the man's shoulder.

It went right through him.

It went right through nothing.

He was gone.

Again.

CHAPTER EIGHT
The Attached Ghost

"Hmm," said Adam. "It's happened again. We should have known he'd take it hard. We should have, like, prepared him or something."

"What are you talking about, Adam?"

"He died again. He had another heart attack and died—just like he did a few minutes ago when he realized he was dead himself."

"He died because he knew he was dead? What are you talking about?"

"See, Molly," said Adam, very patiently, "it's like this. He had a weak heart, right?"

"Right."

"And he's a ghost. Right?"

She had no choice but to agree. "I guess so."

"He is. But if he's a ghost of himself, then wouldn't he have to act like himself?"

"I suppose so."

"So, he still has a weak heart. And we've been shocking him badly—just the way you shocked Dad by shouting like that before."

"But Adam, I didn't, I swear. I was just lying there floating, enjoying the sun, and then Dad came running out."

"Molly, you were shouting, 'Help, help!' It was really scary."

"I swear I wasn't! And when I heard Dad, I looked up and there was this light, and—"

"Light? A really bright light? On the dock?"

"Yes! And it was surrounded by darkness!"

"Like a black hole or something, right?"

"Right! And there seemed to be someone else there, too, inside it."

"A woman, maybe."

"In a long skirt. You saw it, too!"

"I did. But I thought I was just imagining it. And then Dad fell, and Reggie started shouting, and—"

"And you decided not to say anything about it because you thought nobody would believe you." Molly shook her head. "I'm sorry, Adam, I really am. This time, I would have believed you. I would have had to."

"And if I'd told you, I would have believed you about not shouting." He stopped, and then said quietly, "Strange things are happening, Molly."

She nodded. "They really are. Like Granddad here. What were you saying about him?"

"Well, he had a shock when he was still alive, and he died, right? Then a few minutes ago he had a shock when we told him he was dead—and he died. And then, of course, he came back again, right? Because we talked to him after that—and told him about Gram, which was when he died again."

"It is sort of logical," Molly said. A sudden thought struck her. "But if Granddad can die so easily—what about Dad?"

"But Dad doesn't have a weak heart," Adam said.

"No, but even someone with a healthy heart can have a shock and die, can't they?"

Molly was still standing behind the desk, leaning her elbows on the back of the chair and holding her chin as she thought about it all.

"I wish I knew," said Adam. "All I know right now is, if Granddad came back before, he's likely to do it again—any second now. I suggest you move a little to the left."

"Whu—?"

But it was too late. Granddad was back again. He was back, and Molly's elbows were sticking into his shoulders. In fact, Molly could see her arms fuzzily visible through his body, her elbows emerging from the front of his chest. Quickly she pulled her arms back with an involuntary scream. As soon as she'd done that, she apologized to her granddad. "Sorry, it's not like you're scary or repulsive or. . . ." She stopped herself, realizing she was only making things worse. Then she examined her arms for any ghostly blood or guts that might still be clinging to them. They seemed fine, but she gave them a few shakes anyway, just to be safe.

"Don't worry about me," Granddad said, seemingly unaware that he'd just had someone else's arms poking right through him and not really hearing Molly's flustered gibberings. "I'm all right now. It was just . . . well, actually, I don't know what happened."

"I think that you just d—"Adam started to say.

"Never mind, Adam," Molly interrupted. "I mean, sometimes it's better for people if they don't know everything. Right?"

Molly was imagining how she would feel if someone told her she was a ghost and prone to fatal heart attacks. Better Granddad didn't know.

"I suppose so," said Adam. "Never mind, Granddad."

I don't know how a ghost can die, thought Molly. But this one certainly can. And if he can, then what about Dad? She had already been worried before, but now they'd have to watch Dad like hawks. She was tempted to run out to the living room right now to see if he was safe.

"I think I must have fainted," Granddad said. "It's

just so much to take in. I'm sure you can imagine what a shock all of this is for me. I mean, it appears that I'm dead and I didn't even realize it. Good grief!" He shook his head back and forth a few times.

"And," he continued, "my dear wife, Dora. She's gone now as well." He sat in silence for a few moments, looking very miserable, then said, "I hope she had a good life. She did, didn't she?"

Molly nodded. "Yes," she said, "I think she did."

He nodded. "Dora dead," he said, "and me, too, dead also. But then—then why aren't we together?"

Suddenly he stood up and began to shout. "Dora! Dora! Are you there! It's me, Ernest! Dora?"

"Sssh," said Molly. "Calm down!" What if Dad heard and came in to investigate? And saw Granddad? The last thing they needed right now was for Dad to see a ghost—the ghost of his own dead father. It might kill them both—for good!

But Granddad kept right on shouting. "Dora! Dora! I know you must be there! Reveal yourself to me!"

Suddenly, the door burst open.

Oh, no! thought Molly. She didn't want to look. She didn't want to see her father standing in the doorway, a shocked look on his face—a look that would fade as his knees buckled and he sank slowly to the floor.

But it wasn't Dad. It was the nurse. Reggie.

As soon as he stepped into the room, Granddad

stopped shouting. He was, in fact, gone again.

"Who was shouting in here?" Reggie asked, sounding suspicious and cross all at the same time. "You children really are kicking up quite a ruckus. I wish you wouldn't. I've given your father a bit of a sedative, because like I told you before, what he really needs right now is to relax. He'd just dropped off when all the noise started."

He looked very displeased.

"You children do enjoy shouting, don't you?" he said, looking right at Molly.

Adam could see that Molly was terrified. And nothing scared Molly. But somehow, Reggie was even scarier than Granddad. Sure, Granddad was a ghost, and he defied all the rules of logic and the laws of physics. Sometimes he was there and sometimes he wasn't—and even when he was there, he never seemed to be completely there. Look how Molly had got her arms mixed up in him.

But Reggie—well, Reggie was *so* there it was positively alarming. He made Adam feel as wispy as Granddad sometimes looked.

"We're sorry," said Molly, taking a step back. "It was just—just a game we were playing."

"Hmph," said Reggie. "Some game. What was that you were calling? Door?"

"Uh, yes, door. It's . . . it . . . well . . . it. . . ." Molly was in a panic, unable to think of anything.

"It was Thor, actually," said Adam, trying to be very calm. "We were pretending to be ancient Vikings, calling on the gods to help us on our voyage. Oh, Thor, deliver us! Thor is a Viking god, see?"

"I don't care who she is," said Reggie. "Just keep it down." And with that, he shut the door quietly and was gone.

"Who was that?" said Granddad, back again.

"His name is Reggie," said Adam. "Reggie Crankbrain or something. He's a nurse. He's staying next door. He's been looking after—"

"There's something about him, something I don't like," Granddad said. "Just looking at him made me feel weak."

"Really weak, I bet," said Adam. "You disappeared the minute he came into the room."

"I did?"

"You did," said Adam. "I wish I could be invisible when I see him, too. He's very pushy."

"No," said Granddad. "That's not it. I mean, yes, he might well be, as you say, pushy. He does certainly look the type. Those must be size fifteen shoes! But it's not that. It's something else. I feel like I know him—or something about him."

For a moment he was lost in thought. "Oh, well," he finally said. "Enough about that. Right now I have more pressing matters to deal with. Like figuring out where Dora is, my poor, dear Dora." He sniffled a little. "And for that matter," he added, "why I'm here at all."

"I think," Adam said, "it has something to do with the desk."

"My desk?"

"Yes," said Adam, "your desk. Because you were never here before—I mean, at least we never saw you before." He didn't mention the thing he'd seen when they were packing up Gram's house—he wondered if that had been Granddad, too. "But after Gram died last year, we closed up the house in Oxford and Dad and Mom—that's your son Tim, and his wife, our mother—they arranged to have all this stuff sent over here."

"Over here? You mean, we're not in Oxford?"

"No, we're not. We're here in Falcon Lake. It's a couple of hours from our house, an entire ocean away from Oxford—"

"Across the ocean?" Granddad interrupted. "The new world! I always wanted to go to the new world! The majestic Rockies! The magnificent Great Plains! The tractless wilds of the endless northern woods! And now, apparently, here I am!" He looked longingly toward the window, where the pine trees were shaking gently in a light wind. "If only I could go out there and actually experience it!" He sighed. "But as you have seen, I can't."

"But that's just the point," said Adam. "You can't

go out because somehow, you're tied to this desk."

"What I don't understand," Molly said, "is *why* you're here." Maybe, if they could figure that out, they could figure out all the rest—the bright light, the woman in the long dress, maybe even Reggie. And they could keep Dad safe.

Adam gave her an impatient look. "It's the desk, Molly, like I said. It has to be."

"Yes, yes, I can see that," said Molly. "He came with the desk, he's attached to it, he can't leave it, blah blah blah. You're a genius, Adam, I happily admit it. But *why*? Why is here at all?" She gave Granddad an embarrassed look and blushed. "I'm sorry, Granddad," she finally said, "and it's not that I'm not happy to meet you and all, because I am. I guess—I mean I'm happy to see you, even if you are a ghost. But that's the thing. Why are you a ghost?"

"Why?"

"Yes, *why*. I mean, lots of people die, but most of them don't hang around their old furniture, right?"

"I . . . I suppose not," said Granddad. "Although there *was* the case of a cook in Lancashire whose voice often emerged from her old pudding mould after she passed over, exhorting anyone who held it to make sure it never went over 350 degrees Fahrenheit.

Apparently she'd had a serious falling out with her mistress over cracking just such a mould in an over-heated oven, and it scarred her even beyond life."

"Really?" said Adam.

Granddad nodded.

"Cool!" said Adam.

"Cool or not," said Molly, "it's beside the point. I mean, I suppose it's possible that it does some-times happen—but not often, right? I mean, of all the pudding moulds or whatever they are in the world, how many of them are haunted?"

"I only know of the one," said Granddad. "Although there was a toothbrush up in Scotland that liked to sing 'Sweet Adeline,' it's former owner's favourite tune, you see?"

Adam tried to imagine what it would be like to have some dead person's voice coming out of your mouth while you brushed your teeth.

"You could maybe sing along with it," he said. How come Granddad knew all this neat stuff? Adam was really beginning to enjoy having him around.

"Yes!" Granddad chimed in. "A duet for one mouth! You could be in harmony with yourself!"

"Cool!" Adam said again.

"Right on, man, as you youngsters like to say!" added Granddad.

Molly had had enough. This was getting ridicu-lous. All Adam and Granddad were interested in doing was swapping stories! Molly stamped her foot. "Will you two stop changing the subject? This is serious!"

"Sorry, Molly," said Adam.

"Yes, sorry, dear," said Granddad. "What is your point?"

"My point is, most dead people don't hang around after they die. Or if they do, they don't make it obvious to people who are still alive." She was going to remind Granddad of his trouble with getting in touch with Gram, but then realized how cruel that would be. So she didn't say that. Instead, she said, "Why you, Granddad? Why are you, Ernest Barnett, here?"

CHAPTER NINE
The Curse of the Ghost

"Why am I, Ernest Barnett, here. Yes," said Granddad, rubbing his chin with his hand. "Excellent question. And excellent reasoning, dear. Very logical. You remind me of your father."

People were always saying that. It was kind of flattering, because Dad was a smart guy. But being told you were like anyone else, even someone great like Dad, was also very annoying.

"Maybe," said Adam, "it's because you haven't crossed over." Adam had watched enough TV shows about ghosts and aliens to know all there was to know. He even watched ones his father hadn't produced. The ones his father made were always making fun of people who said they saw ghosts. Adam would never tell anybody, of course, but he liked the ones where the people proved that ghosts were real much better.

They seemed much more convincing. And much more imaginative.

Now he was remembering one show where people had talked about ghosts being spirits who were reluctant to leave the earth. "Maybe," he said to Granddad, "you're trapped here on earth until you do something you need to do or figure out something you need to figure out and then you'll cross over."

Molly had seen that program, too. She remembered watching it with Adam and making so many jokes about all the ridiculous things they were saying that Adam had called Mom and complained. Molly thought it was all just a pile of hooey. Irrational nonsense. "Adam," she exclaimed, "this isn't a TV show! This is real."

"Yes, it is," said Adam smugly. "Exactly my point. It is real. He is real. And . . . he's really a ghost!"

He really was. Molly just stood there and said nothing and looked dazed.

"Why *am* I here?" Granddad said again, deep in thought. He paced for a few moments, blinking out as he left the desk and then blinking back in as he came closer to it. All at once, he stopped. "I think I have it!" he said.

"What?" Molly and Adam asked together.

"My mission in life is—" He stopped for a moment, an odd look flitting across his face. "I mean, my mission in life *was* to prove to the world that ghosts exist, that there is another dimension, another realm most of us are not usually aware of."

"Really?" said Adam. "You believe in ghosts! That's fantastic, Granddad!" Finally, someone in the family with a proper imagination! It was about time!

"Hold on a minute, young fellow," said Granddad. "I didn't say I believe in them. I said I spend my time trying to prove they exist. I mean, I hope they do, for if they don't I've wasted a lot of time on them—my entire working life, in fact. And, now, I suppose, death?" He paused for a moment, shaking his head back and forth. "But I won't believe it—really, truly believe it for certain—until I have proof. There must be proof, logical rational, orderly scientific proof! Without proof, it's all just idle speculation, meaningless piffle! The doubters are right! But with proof . . . ! I'll find it if it kills me!"

Perhaps, Molly thought, it already has. Granddad was getting very, very excited—just as he had the last couple of times he died. Maybe that's what happened the first time—the time he really died and became a ghost. And now he was doing it again. They really should get him to calm down.

Molly, though, was having to try hard—very, very hard—to stay calm herself. She took a deep breath and tried to imagine herself throwing a cold glass of water onto her face, the way they did on TV when people started to get hysterical.

"So," Granddad said, "perhaps I was so obsessed with my task when I died that I couldn't let it go. Maybe I'm tied here until I can prove my thesis."

But you are here, Molly thought, so you don't have to. . . . She snorted. It was just all too bizarre.

"What's so funny?" said Adam.

"This!" said Molly, trying to hold back the giggles rising inside her. "All of it! I mean, he wanted to prove ghosts exist, right? Well, I guess he proved it, all right! He *is* the proof! *He* is the ghost he wanted to know about!"

"You're right, Molly!" said Adam. "He is!"

"I am!" said Granddad. "I am a ghost! I exist! And I know I exist because I am the ghost who knows it. I am vindicated!" He paused and then said, "We'll have to get the news out! Inform the authorities! And the press!"

"Dad knows a lot of people who work on the news," said Adam. "He can tell them all about it, and they'll want to come out here and interview you, for sure! Imagine! The first TV interview of a ghost! An actual ghost! It'll be the biggest story in the history of the universe!"

"Yes," Granddad said, "that would be very satisfying. Very gratifying. Go fetch your father, young man!"

What? Molly could hardly believe her ears. Were they both crazy?

"You can't!" she declared. "Adam, come back here."

Adam, who was already halfway to the door, stopped and turned back.

"What's the problem?" he said. "Angry because everyone is going to know you were wrong about ghosts and things all along? Hey, I bet Dad is going to be pretty upset about it, too! Neat!"

"Adam," said Molly, "you're not thinking. Do you *really* want Dad to be upset?"

"Oh, man!" said Adam, suddenly remembering about his father. "You're right. We can't."

"Why not?" said Granddad. "What's the problem?"

Oh no, thought Molly. Now we're going to have to shock him again.

"It's nothing really terrible," she said. "Not really. It's just that he can't walk right. He fell down and hurt his ankle. It's just a sprain, but—"

"Oh, dear. Poor lad. I hope he isn't taking it too hard. And without his mom to comfort him, too. She always knew how to make him feel better."

Adam suddenly had an image in his head of Reggie, holding Dad on his huge lap and singing him a comforting lullaby to make the pain go away.

"It's okay," he said, suppressing a giggle. "He has someone to look after him. That nurse."

"Oh yes," said Granddad, "that's sorted, then. If you're sure you can trust him."

Adam looked at Molly, who looked back at him. If only they *could* be sure.

"But," continued Granddad, "if it's just a sprain, well, surely he can manage to hobble a few steps to see his old Dad. I'd dearly love to see him again."

Granddad, Molly thought, seemed to be determined to have his way. There was no way to get out of it—they would have to tell him about Dad. It might give him another attack, but he could come back again, it seemed, and Dad couldn't. Better to kill an imaginary ghost for the third time than to put her own real live dad in danger.

"The thing is," she said, "we don't want to give Dad a heart attack. I mean, it will be pretty freaky for him to meet you."

"I suppose it would," Granddad said. "Tim never did have much truck with ghosts, poor lad. You could tell he thought I was bonkers to interest myself in them, even though he was just a little lad of six. A very hard-headed fellow, my young Timmie. But why do you worry he'll have a heart attack?"

"Because, well . . . because you did."

"I did?"

"You did. And Dad's thirty-fifth birthday is coming up and, well, we're supposed to make sure nothing bad happens to him," Molly said.

There. She'd said it.

Granddad sat down again. "You are correct, Molly,"

he mused. "I myself have, I mean had, a weak heart. So, it finally got me. Dora always said it would."

Adam was about to tell him he still had the weak heart—and then decided not to.

"And that's not all," Granddad added. "My father died of a heart attack, too," he said. "And for that matter, so did his father, and possibly his father! All just before their thirty-fifth birthdays!"

"Yes, Granddad," said Adam impatiently. "We know all that. That's why we're out here at the lake."

Granddad looked confused. "I don't understand."

"Our dad will be thirty-five tomorrow. And we're worried because—"

"Because all of his ancestors didn't make it past their thirty-fifth birthdays," said Granddad. He sat down, then immediately stood up again. "My little Tim is in danger. That changes everything! We have to stop it from happening." He sat down again. "Could that be why I'm here? To protect Timmie? Did he inherit his weak heart from me? I'd never forgive myself. . . ."

"Well, actually, no, he didn't," said Molly. "At least, we think he didn't. I mean, he's been tested a lot. Mom made him because she was so worried about it. There doesn't seem to be anything wrong with his heart."

93

"Well, that's a relief!"

"But," Molly continued, "Mom isn't totally convinced. She says the family history isn't a good sign and that we have to make sure he doesn't get too excited, no matter what the tests say."

"She sounds like a wise and caring woman, your mother," said Granddad.

"She is," said Molly.

"How wonderful for Timmie." A bewildered look crept across his face. "Good heavens! It's so hard to think of my little six-year-old being married and having children! He started school last year, and he's beginning to learn to ride a bicycle!"

"Yes, Molly," he continued, "you're right to not want to take a chance. I won't ask you to send him to me. It wouldn't be the least bit wise. I don't want him dead the very moment he meets me."

Good, thought Molly, relieved. After all, if she had a bad heart, she'd probably be dead herself already. No doubt about it, seeing a ghost was shocking.

A ghost. Hmmm, she thought. Interesting.

"Granddad, do you remember what happened? Before you died, I mean?"

"As I told you, I was working at my desk," he said. "Why do you ask?"

"Because . . . well, maybe something happened, right? I mean, you didn't suddenly just die for no reason at all. Maybe something happened to scare you."

"Like seeing a ghost," said Adam. "Is that what you mean, Molly?"

Molly nodded.

"Interesting," said Granddad. "Until you two arrived, I was just sitting here, thinking that things were going on pretty much as usual—not even realizing I was dead. But now that you've got me thinking, well, yes—there *was* something!"

"What?" said Adam. Molly waited anxiously for his answer.

"Something. . . ." He looked confused. "Well, something wasn't right."

"Not right?" asked Molly. "How not right?"

Granddad paused, lost deep in thought.

"Well," he finally said, "I do believe I was murdered."

CHAPTER TEN
The Ghost's Secret

Molly shook her head—the same kind of shake she did when water from the lake was caught in her ear. She couldn't believe what she was hearing. No, she thought, it was just too much. For a second, she even felt like she was going to faint.

She'd been having enough trouble accepting all the unbelievable things she'd been forced to believe in the last few hours. Ghosts and mysterious lights and huge, lightning-fast nurses were bad enough. But murder?

I can't take it anymore, she thought. I just can't. I need something normal or I'll go nuts.

"Excuse me," she said politely. And she turned, flung open the door, sprinted down the hall and went back into the living room.

And there was her dad, sitting on the sofa with

his leg up on a stool, chomping on a sandwich as Reggie talked.

"Are you sure," Reggie was saying in his deep, low voice, "you don't want a nice glass of warm milk? It would help you to relax."

Thank heavens, thought Molly. Everything out here seems perfectly normal.

Except for Charlie. She looked under the table in the corner. Charlie wasn't there anymore. That was strange. He always stayed close to Dad whenever he could.

I wonder where he is, thought Molly. Probably just sleeping under a tree somewhere.

Still, Charlie or no Charlie, at least there were no ghosts out here. She smiled. The next thing she'd hear would be Dad telling Reggie where to get off. He never could stand people pushing him around, and Reggie was treating him as if he were about two years old. Plus which, he hated warm milk.

Molly waited. She waited for Dad to tell Reggie that he wasn't a two-year-old. She waited to hear him tell Reggie to mind his own beeswax and leave him alone, thank you.

"Mmm," said Dad dreamily, licking crumbs of bread from his lips, "warm milk! That sounds good. Yes, I believe I'd like some."

Molly was stunned. What was happening to Dad? Did Reggie have him hypnotized or something?

And were things as odd out here as they were in her room?

"And you," said Reggie, turning toward Molly with an angry glare. "Don't you want your sandwich?"

"My sandwich? Oh, yeah, sure."

"Good," said Reggie. "If there's anything I hate it's a food waster! It's almost as rude as getting up and leaving the room in the middle of a meal."

Still deep in thought about her dad's strange behaviour, Molly walked over to the coffee table, took half a sandwich and quickly bit into it.

"I meant . . . ," Reggie pointed at the half eaten sandwich still sitting on Molly's plate.

"Oh," said Molly. She went over and picked that sandwich up, too, and managed to stuff both into her mouth.

I'd like to tell him just where he can go, thought Molly. But there was something about him—something she couldn't quite put her finger on. It wasn't just his size, either, but somehow, he managed to make her feel like a cringing coward. And normally, she wasn't afraid of anybody or anything!

And what about Dad? What was wrong with him? Was he afraid of Reggie, too? Afraid enough to actually drink warm milk? Reggie was in the kitchen already, pouring milk into a saucepan and putting it onto the burner. And Dad was just sitting there like a baby and letting Reggie run his life. It was definitely not normal. It was almost as upsetting as the whole business with Granddad and the murdering ghosts.

There had to be a logical explanation. An alternate universe? String theory? Someone had spiked the drinking water? No, not even Adam would believe any of that. Wait! she thought. There is an explanation! This is a dream! I'm dreaming it all! I've probably fallen asleep on my bed and I'll wake up any minute!

She grinned. That had to be it. She felt better already.

"You know what, Dad?" she said. "I'm dreaming!"

"What?" he said. "What did you say, Molly?"

"I'm dreaming right now," she exclaimed. "I bet you haven't even sprained your ankle. I probably fell asleep before that. And that means that the big hulk," she pointed to Reggie, who again had a knife in his hand and a sour look on his face, "doesn't even exist. He just represents some horrible trauma or something from my past that I've buried in my subconscious! Although I can't figure out what, exactly—something to do with a bad experience with an elephant in a garden, maybe? If I had an imagination, I'd say he was a figment of it!" Suddenly she had an idea. She looked right at Reggie, squeezed her lips together, and blew.

"Blblblblblbl!" she said. "Take that, figment!" It felt so good that she pressed her lips together and blew again.

From the kitchen, Reggie shot her a look that could kill. And yet she didn't die. It had to be a dream!

"Molly," said her father angrily. "You are being very rude. And childish."

"Don't be silly, Dad," she said. "How can I be rude when I'm sleeping. I think I'll have another sandwich—maybe I'll have three more sandwiches. They're very tasty. For a figment, he's an excellent cook. And if I'm dreaming, it can't be bad for me, right?"

"Molly," Dad said. "You're wide awake." He turned to Reggie. "Please forgive her, Reggie. I don't know what's gotten into her. She's usually much more sensible. And much more polite."

"Really?" said Reggie, his voice icy.

"Well, of course you'd say that!" she told Dad. "You're part of my dream, after all."

And if the whole thing was just a dream, she could go back and deal with Granddad again, and with his silly idea about murdering spirits. It wasn't real, so there was nothing to be scared about. Granddad himself was just a part of the dream, too—and so was the imaginary Adam in there with him. She turned and ran down the hall back to the Wonder Woman room.

When I get there, she told herself, Adam will probably have turned into a giant carrot or something, and Granddad will be playing the tuba and tap-dancing on six pairs of legs.

But when she got to the room and walked past

the boxes to the desk, it was just the same old Adam. Adam and the Granddad ghost. And they weren't dancing or growing green tops, either. They were just chatting away like old friends.

Which scared Molly more than carrots and tap-dancing.

Which proved to her that it *was* a nightmare.

"And I hate bugs," Adam was saying, "don't you? Especially leeches. But we need to be here with Dad to make sure he doesn't meet the same fate you did." He turned to Molly. "Where did you go?"

"I left to see if this was all real," she replied. "I've decided I'm dreaming."

"I said that *I* was dreaming," Adam objected, "before, when I . . . well, when I fainted, remember? And you told me to shut up!"

"Yes," said Molly impatiently. "Of course I did. I told you to shut up because I didn't get it then. I didn't realize then that this is *my* dream. Which it is, obviously. I'm so glad I finally figured it out! I thought I was losing my mind! And anyway," she added, giving Adam a scrunched-up frown, "shut up! Shut up, creepo! There! I can say anything I want in my own dream."

"Creepo?" said Adam. "You can say anything you want and you're calling me a creepo?"

As if he could think up anything better. Anyway, she didn't care. With any luck this pretend Adam would just wither up and go away altogether, along with the pretend Granddad ghost. And the figment hulk nurse. And the real non-creepo Adam would come back. And she could go back to floating in the lake.

"I'm sorry, young lady," said Granddad. "But I don't believe this is a dream."

"Well, you wouldn't," she said, "because you're part of it, too, right? You're all just products of my overactive imagination."

"Hah!" said Adam. "That proves it isn't a dream. Since when do you have an overactive imagination?"

Yeeks, thought Molly. *That* was true. Even her dreams were practical and had a sort of logic to them. This had no logic at all.

"Molly," her grandfather said patiently, "this must be a terrible shock to you—I can see why you would be confused. But I think I can solve the problem. I'll prove to you that you're awake. But how?"

He thought for a minute. "I know," he finally said. "Pinch her, Adam!"

"Gladly," said Adam. And he did. A big pinch on the arm.

"Ouch," said Molly. "That hurt!"

"Good," said Adam. "You deserve it for calling me a creepo. How lame."

"If it hurt," said Granddad, "then you must be awake."

"Maybe," said Molly. "Or maybe my subconscious

wants me to be hurt! Maybe I'm punishing myself for something. I wonder what?"

"For just being yourself, probably," said Adam, standing back so that Molly wouldn't be able to pinch him in return. "Now what, Granddad?"

"I know," said Granddad. "Molly, I'll tell you something that only your dad and I would know. Then you go and ask him about it. If he gives you the correct answer, you'll know that I'm quite real—or at least as real as a ghost can be."

That did seem logical. Molly agreed. It was worth a try.

"But—" Adam hardly had his mouth open when Molly interrupted him.

"What now, creepo?" Molly said.

"Oh. Nothing," he said. "Never mind." Adam had been about to say that if Molly was dreaming everything, then why couldn't she dream what Granddad would say while she was out of the room? But if she insisted on calling him stupid names, well, too bad. Anything to get her to stop this, even if it wasn't the least bit logical. So much for *her* being the rational one. He gave her a big fake smile.

Molly didn't even notice. She was too busy hoping and praying Granddad was wrong. If he was right and she really was awake, she would be extremely embarrassed. What would Dad think of her awful behaviour? And what would Reggie do about it?

And as for calling Adam a creepo. . . . She felt herself blushing in embarrassment. Name calling was never acceptable in the Barnett household, even lame names like creepo.

She thought for a moment about things only Dad and Granddad would know. "It has to be something I couldn't possibly know already. It can't be anything I might have seen when we went to England to visit Gram. It has to be something that's not even in my subconscious. And something Dad wouldn't have told us."

"I know," Granddad said. "Ask your father what our secret password was when he was little."

"Secret password?" asked Adam, very interested. "Why did you have a secret password?"

"It was a game we played," said Granddad. "I had to say it before Timmie would let me into his tree house."

"But he could have mentioned that to us," Molly countered.

"I doubt it," said Granddad. "After all, it was a secret."

Molly still wasn't sure.

"Maybe Gram would have said something about it to us?"

"I don't think so," Granddad said. "I don't recall ever talking to her about it. It was a special thing just between me and Timmie."

"Okay," said Molly.

"I'll tell Adam what it is once you've left the room," said Granddad. "That way, you'll know I'm not just agreeing with whatever he says to persuade you. Off you go."

Molly nodded. Once again she made the short trip down the hall and found her father and Reggie just as she left them.

Or—not quite as she'd left them. Reggie was standing behind Dad now, that big knife still in his hand. But now, instead of using it to slice sandwiches and pickles, Reggie had it raised above his head, it's shiny, silver blade glinting in a sunbeam that was coming through the window.

"Dad!" said Molly, alarmed. "Watch out!"

Reggie immediately lowered the knife and smiled—a very fake looking smile.

"Yes," he said, "now that the light is on it I can see that it does need to be washed again. Thought so." He gave Molly another phony grin and headed toward the sink.

"Molly," Dad said, "What on earth are you thinking? Shouting? Again?"

"Sorry, Dad."

"Honestly, Molly. First pretending you were drowning, and now all this. We need to have a talk, young lady."

The look her father was giving her was not

pleasant, and Reggie, holding the knife under the tap, looked even more menacing. If looks could kill, she'd be dead twice. If her unconscious was punishing her in this dream, she must have done something really awful.

If it *was* a dream.

"Yeah, Dad, sure," she said. "But first, please, there's something I need to know."

His look turned even darker. "Well?"

"Do you remember having a secret password when you were little? Something that your father had to say before you let him into your tree house?"

"Good grief!" he said, "I haven't thought about that in years. How did you know about it?"

For a moment, she tried to think of an explanation that might make sense to him, but then quickly gave up and said, "Please, just tell me. What was it? Do you remember?" .

"Yes," he said. "As it happens, I do. It was Barnett Bonkers."

"I'll be right back," she said, as she turned and rushed down the hall.

She pushed open the bedroom door and blurted out the answer.

"Barnett Bonkers!" she exclaimed.

"That's exactly what he told me," Adam said, delighted. It was about time Molly realized she wasn't in any stupid dream.

But Molly still wasn't convinced—or at least she was trying to talk herself out of being convinced.

"If I am dreaming, I could have made all this up, too! All of it! I could have just dreamed Granddad! And the light, and Dad's ankle! And Reggie holding that knife over Dad, all of it!"

"Reggie doing what?" said Adam. Okay, that was it. That was the last straw.

"Molly!" Adam shouted in frustration, "you aren't dreaming! Granddad just said he might have been murdered. We have a stranger out there, apparently holding a knife over Dad! We need to figure out who killed Granddad and why! It could be important!" He paused. "You would tell us if Reggie was still holding a knife over Dad, wouldn't you?"

"Yes, of course I would, and no he's not," she answered. And then she collapsed onto the bed, defeated. "Okay," she said. "I give up. It's real. Now what?"

CHAPTER ELEVEN
The Ghost Who Died

"We need to think," Adam said. "About Granddad being murdered."

"Murdered," their granddad repeated thoughtfully. "Yes, I was, I know I was. But I can't remember how, exactly. Yet for some reason, I'm certain it happened. This could be important!"

"Tell me," said Molly. "What's the last thing you remember?"

"Good question, my dear," their granddad said. "If I'm dead, something must have killed me—something got me into this pickle. And that something ought to be the last thing I remember. Very logical indeed." He thought for a moment.

"I was frightened," he finally said. "Yes, I remember I was very frightened. But of what? It eludes me at the moment." He smacked the desk with his hand.

"Why can't I remember?" He suddenly stood up. "I have to remember. A life is in the balance—the life of my own son! We must save him. We must!"

"Maybe we can," Adam said, still surprisingly calm.

"What do you mean, Adam?" Molly asked impatiently, "Maybe we can what?"

"Maybe we can save Dad," he said. "With Granddad's help."

Molly glared at him. "Are you completely nuts?" she said. "Dad can't know anything about Granddad. I mean, imagine, if he walked in here and saw. . . . No, it can't happen!"

"I didn't mean Dad had to *see* Granddad, Molly," said Adam. "What kind of fool do you think I am?"

Molly began to speak, but Adam stopped her with an angry look. "Don't answer that."

"I'm not saying anything," she told him. "But what do you mean?"

"Yes, what do you mean, lad?" said Granddad.

"Well, the thing is, we know things now that Granddad didn't know before he died. We know them because he's here. We know them because we know why he died."

"We do?" said Molly. "But he can't remember—"

"He doesn't have to remember, Molly, because we've seen it."

"We have?"

"Yes. Twice." He turned from Molly to Granddad. "I'm sorry, Granddad, but you have to be told. You've died twice more since you've been here."

"I've——? What——? What are you talking about, lad?"

"You got very upset, twice. The first time was when we told you that you were dead, and the second was——well, when we told you about Gram."

"Yes, I remember being upset. Very upset. But dead? Are you sure?"

"Pretty sure. You grabbed at your chest, and you had trouble breathing——and then, well, you just disappeared."

"But it wasn't permanent," Molly interjected, worried about how Granddad was going to take this bizarre news. "You came back again, almost right away."

"Yes," said Adam, "you did. Whatever it is that's got you tied to this desk, it's strong, very strong. It's not letting you go, even if you die again."

"Fascinating!" Granddad said. "I've never heard of a ghost who died again after the first time. I must write a paper about it. I'm sure the gentlemen in the Society for Psychical Research will be most interested."

"The Society for Psychical Research?" Adam repeated.

"It's a group of scholars and others that studies

ghosts," Granddad explained. "I am a member," he said proudly. "I'm actually the vice president."

"I see," said Adam.

I bet they would be interested in that paper, Molly told herself—especially because it would be the first paper ever published that was actually written by a ghost. It would really be ghost-written!

"Anyways," Adam said, trying to get the conversation back on track, "you died when you got excited and upset—so that must be what did it the first time."

"That is logical," Granddad said.

"Yes, it is," Molly agreed. "Sort of. But so what?"

"So," said Adam, "that means it wasn't just a random heart attack. At least, that's what I think. I mean, if it happened to Granddad, and if it happened to *his* father and *his* father and *his* father, all at the same time in their lives, then something must have made it happen. Something that upset Granddad enough to make him die—because he thinks he was murdered."

"I suppose so," said Molly. "But the same person couldn't have killed all of them. I mean, Granddad died thirty years ago, and his father must have died about thirty years before that, and his father thirty years before that, and so on. We're talking about more than a hundred years! You can't seriously be suggesting that the same person killed them all—and might be trying to kill Dad now?"

"No," said Adam. "Not a person. At least, not a living person."

"A spirit!" Granddad said. "It has to be a spirit! A ghost killed us all!"

CHAPTER TWELVE
Ghosts that Kill

Ghosts that kill. Eerie. I wonder why, thought Adam. They must have had a reason—some grudge against the Barnett family that made them want to get rid of all the sons before they became thirty-five. Was it something one of his ancestors did to someone? Was it something to do with revenge, or politics, or money?

Oh my gosh, Adam thought. I'm a son, too! If this continues, it'll be my turn next—and I have only about twenty-five years left of my life.

But first, it would have to be Dad's turn.

Dad!

"I think I'd better go check on Dad," he said, and he was out of the room and down the hall before Molly or Granddad could say anything.

Dad seemed to be okay. Just sleeping on the

couch. The room was empty otherwise. Reggie must have gone back to the Rosen's for something.

There was, though, a strange noise coming from the door. A kind of ghostly noise, like chains rattling or—

Or a dog wanting to come in! Adam went over and opened the door and let Charlie through. He immediately zoomed past Adam, hopped onto the sofa, crawled onto Dad's chest, and licked his face.

Dad didn't even move. Maybe he wasn't sleeping after all. Maybe he was . . . Adam had to check. He went over and gingerly touched his dad's neck. Yes, there was a pulse. Dad was alive. But he sure was sleeping deeply.

Charlie curled up beside him and closed his eyes. Well, at least things were quiet. Adam went back down the hall.

"That surprises me, Molly," Granddad was saying as Adam came into the room. "You never considered that ghosts might exist? Did your father never tell you about my work?"

"Yes," Molly answered. "In fact the film he's making right now is about haunted theatres in the city."

Granddad beamed. "There you go! A chip off the old block."

"And," Molly continued, "how they aren't really haunted. How ghosts are a bunch of nonsense and there has never been any proof of their existence." She paused. "He's just as sure about that as I am. I think he believed you sort of . . . wasted . . . well, you should have used your time better."

Granddad shook his head. "So Timmie grew up a skeptic?" he said. "Dear me. Well, of course, children do often rebel against their parents—and he always was determined to be logical. You know, I believe he almost independently invented Archimedes' principle again all by himself, playing with a plastic cup in his bath when he was a baby!"

"Archimedes' principle?" said Adam. "What's that?"

"Any body partially or completely submerged in a fluid," said Granddad, "is buoyed up by a force equal to the weight of the fluid displaced by the body."

"Oh," said Adam.

"Honestly," said Granddad. "Don't they teach you young folk anything at school these days?" Then he turned to Molly. "You know, dear, if you're as logical as you say, you really ought to accept that you're not in a dream."

"Why?"

"Because it's the only logical thing to do, once you accept the basic premise that spirits might exist. Once you admit that single possibility, everything else follows."

"It does?" said Molly.

"Yes, it does. For instance, can you see me?"

"Well, yes."

"Can you talk with me?"

"Yes. I'm doing it, aren't I?"

"And can you wake up?"

"Well, no." She shook her head violently, but nothing happened.

"If Granddad is right," said Adam, "it would also account for you shouting like that. Before, when Dad fell."

"It would?"

"Sure. I mean, you say you didn't do it. But Dad and I heard you clearly. Maybe a spirit took over your mind and controlled your voice. I saw it happen on a TV show once."

Ew, thought Molly. That was a disgusting thought.

But it did seem sort of logical.

Adam and Molly quickly filled Granddad in on what had happened on the dock.

"I see," said Granddad, "Very interesting. There are many examples of events like that in the literature—often involving young girls like Molly. There was one in Surrey some years back involving a young lady who suddenly started speaking in a deep, masculine voice, shouting about vengeance against someone named Rodney. In the middle of it, she thrust her arm through a window and shattered the glass—but when she calmed down, there wasn't the slightest scratch on her arm! Adam, my boy, this is fascinating. Tell me again exactly what happened? What did you hear?"

"I heard Molly scream as if she were really in trouble," Adam said. "But you know, come to think of it, I didn't *see* her scream. I only heard it. So maybe the spirit can make the sound without taking over her body."

As Adam and Granddad continued to talk, Molly sat where she was and thought about the whole episode. It would be nice to believe that that was what had happened—that despite what Dad and Adam and Reggie said, it wasn't her, that she hadn't actually screamed. It would mean they were right when they said they'd heard something—and that she was right, too. It was perfectly logical.

If, that is, you accepted the existence of ghosts. Like Granddad said. If you accepted that, everything else made perfect sense.

Adam certainly seemed fine with it all. He and Granddad were happily involved in a conversation about ghostly matters. Right now, Adam was telling Granddad about how his friend Tad was convinced there was a ghost haunting the basement of the brand new house he just moved into, and Granddad was suggesting that the house could have been built on an ancient graveyard and hence could in fact be the subject of ghostly apparitions.

Maybe, Molly thought, she should behave as if it were all real. If she did finally wake up, no harm was done.

"If Timmie is as much of a skeptic as you say,"

Granddad said, "then that's another reason not to tell him about me. I certainly don't want to upset him enough to harm his health."

"Do you think we're right, then?" Adam asked anxiously. "I mean, do you *really* think he's in danger?"

"If what happened to me and my father and his father are any indication, then I would say yes, he's very much in danger."

"But then—can't you see things from where you are? Things that could help us protect him?" Adam asked hopefully.

Granddad sighed. "I wish I could. But unfortunately, I seem to have a very limited view, specifically, this room and the view outside that window. If there are spirits here, I'm certainly not seeing them. Except," he put his hand up in front of his face, "except myself, of course. No, I'm afraid I've never been lucky enough to actually experience a spirit—although I've often had the sense that one was there, just beyond my ken, calling out to me."

"Kidlets!" It was a voice from the other side of the cottage. "Are you there?"

Granddad leaped up. "But perhaps I've just heard a spirit! I could swear I just heard my father say 'kidlet'! That's what he always called out when he wanted me."

CHAPTER THIRTEEN
Ghostwriting

"That's not a spirit, Granddad," said Molly, who also recognized the voice. "It's Dad."

"And," added Adam, "he's still alive. As far as I know."

"Molly? Adam? Are you there?"

"He's coming down the hall!" whispered Molly, listening at the door. "His footsteps are getting closer!"

"He can't see Granddad," said Adam. "He'll freak out for sure!"

There was just one thing to do, Molly thought. "Granddad! Come over here! Now!"

"What?"

"Away from the desk!"

"Oh! Yes, of course."

He disappeared just as Dad opened the door. Charlie, who was with him, rushed into the room towards the desk. Then, suddenly, he stopped. He whined, turned once, and slunk back out the door, his tail between his legs.

"What's going on in here?" Dad looked and sounded a little groggy. "I thought I heard a strange voice."

"Uh . . . it was just us, Dad," said Molly. "Playing a game."

"Thor," said Adam. "We were pretending to be Viking gods! 'Thor deliver us!'"

"Whatever," said Dad, "but I wish you'd keep it down a little. There's been way too much shouting around here today," he added, giving Molly a meaningful look. Suddenly, his face changed. "What's that?"

"What?" said Molly, alarmed. Dad was looking over her shoulder, where the gap between the piles of boxes gave a clear view of the desk. She turned in time to catch sight of Granddad just before he disappeared again.

"There's nothing there," she said.

"Nothing at all," Adam added, moving between the piles of boxes to block the view.

But there would be any second now, he thought. Granddad was bound to pop back into view—he didn't seem to have any choice about it. No matter how many times he tried to leave the desk, he was always back again a moment later.

It must be giving him a terrible headache, thought Adam.

And it was very dangerous. They had to get Dad out of the room. Immediately.

"Strange," said Dad, "for a minute there I could have sworn I saw someone behind that old desk." He rubbed his eyes. "It must be these pills Reggie gave me."

"You should have another nap," said Adam, holding his t-shirt out from the sides so that it blocked as much of the view as possible.

"Yes," said Molly, taking Dad's arm and guiding him out the door. "Adam's right. A nap would be an excellent idea. And you're not supposed to be using that ankle."

"You're right," he said. "Another nap is an excellent idea. I'm going across the hall to have one right now. That's what I was coming to tell you."

"Oh," said Molly, "good."

"When Reggie comes back," Dad said, "tell him I'm in the bedroom." And with that, he shuffled across the hall and was gone.

"My Timmie!" their granddad said as he appeared again, a big smile on his face. "A grown man! He's very handsome!"

"He looks just like you," said Adam.

Who knew ghosts could blush?

"Nevertheless," their granddad reiterated. "I do think he's handsome. A father's prejudice, I suppose."

"I'm so glad he's having a nap," said Molly,

anxiously approaching the desk again. "It'll give us some time to figure out what to do." And it'll keep him away from Reggie for a while. What was it about Reggie that was so unsettling, outside of his gigantic size? Even Charlie seemed to feel it. Come to think of it, he slunk about and whined every time Reggie was in the room.

"Molly is right," Granddad said. "I believe we have a mission. It's up to the three of us to ensure that your father doesn't meet the same fate as the rest of the males in my family."

"But how?" she said.

For a moment there was silence. Finally, Adam spoke. "What I think is, we should start by doing what Granddad said earlier. We should start with the idea that ghosts exist. It's the only logical thing to do."

"I suppose so," said Molly. It was totally ridiculous, but she couldn't think of an alternative. She'd have to go along with it for now—and be on the lookout for other more sensible explanations. Anything to protect Dad.

"And," Adam added, "that probably means Granddad was right when he said he thought it was a ghost who deliberately scared him to death."

"It was cold-blooded murder," said Granddad. "At least it would have been, if spirits had blood."

"The only safe thing for us to do," Adam continued,

"is to assume that the same spirit or spirits are out to get Dad, too. Our enemy is a ghost!"

"Well, then," said Molly, gritting her teeth and forcing herself to go along with the idea. "I have to ask the same question I asked before: Why? Granddad, do you have any idea why all the men in our family for so many generations have died like this? And why did it happen just before their thirty-fifth birthdays?"

"Good questions," said Granddad. "Exactly the kind of strict, intellectual rigour with which I've always tried to approach these problems myself."

"And——?" asked Molly impatiently.

"I don't know. Not yet, at any rate. I've been wondering about that very question ever since I first learned of the family history. It was after my father died, when I was a mere lad like Adam. I made a point of gathering all the family papers and other records I could find, and I've searched and searched for clues. But so far, I've had no luck. Or——wait a minute!"

"What is it?" said Adam.

"I was going over some of those old family papers just before I——just before it happened. And you know, come to think of it, I believe I was on to something! Yes, I was! I know I was! If only I could remember what!" He put his hands on the sides of his head, lost in his own thoughts.

He has to remember, thought Adam. He glanced

around the room, looking for something, anything that might help them.

The boxes! Of course!

"Do you think it might be in these papers?" he asked, pointing to them. "They're the ones you had in your study in Oxford. Gram kept them just the way they were when you died, and Mom arranged to have them sent here along with the desk so she and Dad could go through them."

"I see," said Granddad, nodding. "But I've been working on them all morning—I mean, I was working on them *that* morning. The papers I'm talking about are probably on my desk."

"But there are no papers on your desk," Molly said.

"Then what am I working on?" Granddad asked. He reached down to the desk and appeared to be lifting something up—something invisible. But as he lifted it up off the desk, it came into view. "What about these?" he said.

Molly and Adam stared at the papers, not quite believing what they'd just seen. Adam reached out and snatched the papers from Granddad's hand. As he pulled them toward him, they disappeared from view.

"I thought so!" said Adam, flinging his arms in the air triumphantly. "Those are ghostly papers!"

"Be careful, Adam!" said Granddad. "You almost

ripped them. And now you've sent them flying all over the place. Can you pick them up, please? They must be there somewhere on the floor on your side of the desk."

Adam bent down to the floor—and saw nothing. He moved his hand back and forth across the floor, hoping to feel the papers. Still nothing. Molly was down on her knees now, too, hands brushing the floor, encountering nothing but the occasional grain of sand.

"No luck, Granddad," she finally said. "We can't see them or feel them, so we don't know whether we've found them or not. Can you come over here? Maybe you can find them."

Granddad inched around the desk, keeping one hand firmly on its surface. When he got to the front, he kneeled down, hand still touching the desk.

"Here's one," he said, lifting his free hand to show a page. "And I can see one just over there. . . ." He reached out, out, until only his fingertips were attached to the desk.

And then he was gone. He appeared again, almost immediately, in the chair behind the desk.

"I can see them but I can't get to them," he said.

"And we can get to them," said Molly, "but we can't see them or pick them up."

"I'm sure the answers we needed were in those papers," said Granddad glumly.

"Nice one, Adam," Molly said.

Adam felt sick.

"Don't be too hard on your brother, Molly," said Granddad. "He didn't know what he was doing. He merely wanted to understand."

"Yeah," she added, still angry. "And he's stopped us from *ever* being able to understand. Now what?"

"The boxes!" Adam suddenly said.

"What?" said Molly. "What are you on about now?"

"We've lost the ghost papers," said Adam. "Well, actually, *I* lost the ghost papers. But Gram must have picked them up, afterwards, you know, and put them away with all the rest of Granddad's stuff. The real papers, those ones I just lost, could be in these boxes."

"You know," said Granddad, looking much more cheerful, "you must be right. Don't you think so, Molly?"

Molly nodded. Once more, she had to admit it did seem logical. If you accepted that ghosts of papers could exist in the first place.

Which she had just seen.

Which she therefore had to accept.

"In which case," Granddad said, "we need to go through those boxes."

"I'm on it," said Adam enthusiastically, ripping the tape off the box nearest to him and pulling the flaps open. He reached inside and picked up a piece of paper from the top of the large stack inside.

And that's when the horror began.

CHAPTER FOURTEEN
Ghostly Horror

There was, Adam could see, a tiny spider crawling on the sheet of paper he'd pulled out of the box. Nothing to get alarmed at. Not really. Just a very small one.

Trying not to think about touching it, Adam gingerly brushed the spider off the paper, and then looked around nervously to be sure it hadn't landed on him. There was nothing he hated more, out of all the bugs he hated, than spiders.

But to be fair, it was really tiny. And it seemed to be gone. He looked back down at the paper.

Crawling, not on the paper, but on his hand, was a huge brown daddy-long-legs.

Adam shrieked and shook his hand violently. The spider fell off and landed on the floor. As he looked down to figure out where it was going, he saw a stream of spiders pour over the top of the box.

Spiders! Hundreds of spiders! They scrambled

down to the floor, heading straight for his feet, his flipflops offering him no protection at all! Screaming, Adam jumped away.

It made no difference. Now a black spider the size of a tarantula was scampering up his leg, followed by assorted brown spiders—the kind Adam knew were poisonous. Now they had reached the top of his shorts and were crawling inside his clothes. Now the screams were stuck in his throat.

He tried desperately to brush the bugs off and saw that, somehow, there were also spiders all over his arms—an army of spiders in motion!

They were crawling onto his chest now, and he could feel them in his hair and on his face. They were everywhere, everywhere! They were even crawling into his eyes. Adam was in a paroxysm of fear and terror, jumping and slapping and gasping for breath. He thought he was going to die from the sheer horror. He tried to close his eyes to keep the spiders out, but it was too late. His eyelids caught on spiders and refused to close. And he could feel something crawling into his ears, too. That was too much to bear.

"Help! Help me!" Adam called out. Why wasn't Molly doing something? Why wasn't she helping him? Were they all over her, too?

"Is everything all right in here?" It was Reggie. He was standing at the open door. As Reggie's deep voice rumbled through the room, suddenly Adam's eyes were clear. He looked down. The spiders were gone. Gone. In a split second they'd disappeared. It made no sense, but Adam was so relieved that for the moment he couldn't have cared less. He brushed his arms and ran his hands through his hair, making sure there was nothing awful there as his glance darted from the floor to the box and back again, and then, finally, to Molly.

She was staring at him, wide-eyed.

"What was all that screaming about?" said Reggie.

Adam couldn't speak. He was still too terrified to think straight.

"He was pretending," Molly jumped in. "He was pretending that—"

"That spiders were crawling all over me!" Adam managed to get out. "And who was pretending?"

"Spiders?" Reggie asked. "Really? Were you pretending or not?"

To Molly, it looked as if Reggie had a smile on his face. A small one, but a smile nevertheless. It was odd.

"It's . . . it's part of that game we were playing." Molly answered before Adam could. She wished she had enough imagination to make up something believable and to get Reggie out of there. "That game about . . . what was it again, Adam?"

He was looking dazed. She gave him a jab in the arm.

"The name of the *game*, Adam. Where you *pretend* there are spiders, remember?" She jabbed him again.

"Ouch," said Adam, "stop that. Molly, I wasn't—"

"Thor!" Molly suddenly remembered. "It was about Thor. He's a Viking or something, I think. Yes, a Viking. And we're doing the part where he . . . uh . . . where he fights his epic Viking battle with the giant spiders!"

Boy, Molly told herself, that sounded lame.

And Adam was just looking confused.

But miraculously, Reggie bought it. "Giant spiders, eh?"

"Yes! Huge ugly ones, with . . . with . . . uh, thick hairy feelers full of scary muscles and beady glaring eyes and evil down-turned mouths and huge square jaws and—." Oops. Her description of the spiders had somehow turned into a description of Reggie himself. She'd better just shut up, right now.

"It was Adam's idea," she said, just to be safe. And anyway, Adam deserved whatever he got! She was furious with him for scaring her with that screaming. What had he been thinking? What if Dad had woken up and run in here and seen Granddad and had a heart attack? She would wring Adam's neck, just as soon as Reggie left.

"Spiders with huge square jaws!" said Reggie. "Probably crawling over everything, I bet. You certainly do have a wicked imagination, young man."

"But I wasn't imag—" Adam still couldn't take it all in.

"And you really do need to control it." He narrowed his eyes, giving Adam a threatening look. "I see that your father is having a nap. It would not be a good thing if you woke him up—not a good thing at all. Understand?"

Just what I was thinking, thought Molly.

"I'm going now," added Reggie. "I'm going to go sit in the living room and read my knitting magazine."

Reggie read knitting magazines? What was he planning to make, some cozy holders for his knives? As he waved the magazine in front of Molly's face, she had a fleeting vision of a fuzzy pink turtleneck sweater with a cuddly teddy bear knitted into it.

As soon as Reggie closed the door, Molly turned to Adam.

"Are you crazy?" she exclaimed.

"What do you mean?"

"Why were you screaming like that?" Molly said. "It was bad enough that Reggie came in—it could have been Dad!"

"Molly!" Adam declared. "I was covered in spiders! They were all over me! Didn't you see them?"

"All I could see was a bunch of dusty papers," Molly said. "You and your ridiculous imagination!"

"It wasn't his imagination," Granddad said. "I saw them, too."

Molly and Adam turned to him. "What?" said Molly.

"I saw them clear as day," Granddad said. "I had to hide behind the desk when that huge fellow came in but until then I could see them perfectly."

"How could you?" said Molly, perplexed. "They weren't there."

"Some might say that I'm not here either," he said. "But you can see *me*."

"I don't understand," said Adam. His heart was still thudding in his chest. He was sweating. He felt faint again. What had just happened?

"I believe we just witnessed a dark, supernatural event," said Granddad. "And, you know, I wonder if it's similar to the one that frightened me to death."

"I can believe that," said Adam, "because honestly, if it hadn't stopped when it did I think I might have died of fright."

"There's no question about it now," said Granddad. "There is certainly a dark force at work here—and we need to figure out what it is before something worse happens. And that fellow—the big, ugly one with the nice shirt?"

"Reggie," said Molly.

"Reggie, is it? Hmmm." Granddad paused, lost in thought. "Well, anyway," he continued, "it's not just that he gives me a bad feeling, even though he certainly does. There's something else, too. . . ."

"What?" said Molly.

"I don't know! It's there, just at the edge of my thoughts."

Well, thought Molly, that's it, then. As long as it was at the edge of his thoughts it wasn't going to help them. It was time to act, not a time to sit around waiting and talking.

"There's nothing else to do," she said. "We'll need to take a look at those papers."

"No!" said Adam, terrified, "We can't!"

"Don't worry, Adam," she said. "I'll do it this time. I'm not afraid of spiders, so the dark forces can send as many as they want, I don't care!"

And anyway, she told herself, I didn't see them the last time—there's no way I'm superstitious enough to see them now.

"Very brave," said Granddad with approval.

"I'm brave, too," Adam objected. "I just hate bugs." He stopped to think for a moment and then added, "And leeches and bats and snakes and—"

"I didn't mean to imply that you aren't brave," Granddad said quickly.

"It's just that I can picture all the gross things that can happen because I'm always imagining stuff and. . . ."

Molly didn't want to listen to Adam rant on about his imagination. He always had an excuse for being a wuss. She was sick of hearing it. Seemed to her it was all just a way to get out of work that needed to be done.

"I'm thinking," Adam would say when it was time for chores. Guess what? Thinking doesn't unpack the dishwasher or clear the table, as she had often pointed out to him as he stood in the middle of the kitchen, a plate in his hand and a blank look on his face.

Molly stepped up to the box, took a deep breath, and peered in.

And that's when the horror happened to Molly.

All at once, the entire room seemed to move inwards, getting smaller and smaller and darker and darker until Molly was alone in a tiny, pitch-black space. It was then that she started to scream. There was one thing and one thing only that terrified Molly, and that was small spaces. When she was five years old, she had accidentally locked herself in the tiny downstairs bathroom and it had taken what felt like forever for her parents to get her out. Ever since, she'd been claustrophobic.

It was, of course, irrational. Completely irrational. There was nothing to be afraid of—not really. Her mind was playing tricks on her.

Be calm, she told herself. Be calm. Think. Be logical.

With great effort, Molly took stock of the situation. Her heart was racing. She was gasping for breath. She had no feeling in her arms or legs. She was terrified! Completely terrified! *Let me out. Oh, please please please let me out let me out let me out.*

But the walls actually seemed to be getting closer now. She tried to move, and she couldn't do it. It was like there was another skin just over her skin. But it didn't move like skin—it resisted her every motion. It was as if she had suddenly gone blind and become completely encased in concrete.

Let me out let me out let me out.

She was being squeezed now, like in a vice.

Let me out let me out let me out.

Where was Adam? She couldn't see him—couldn't see anything but blackness. Couldn't smell anything.

Couldn't feel anything but the sensation of being squeezed all over.

How could this be happening? It was impossible. It was awful, awful.

Letmeoutletmeoutletmeout.

Without even realizing she was doing it, she started to yell for her dad. "Dad! Dad!"

And then—

It was gone.

It was gone and Reggie was standing over her, shaking her. She was in her room, Adam was there beside Reggie, and both of them were staring at her. She panted for air, her heart beating wildly.

"Molly," Reggie said, his huge hands holding her arms and shaking her so hard she could feel her bones rattling against each other. "Can you hear me? Molly?"

"Ouch," she said. "Stop it! You're going to break something."

"Ah!" said Reggie. "There you are at last." He gave her a few more shakes before he let go.

Molly's brains felt scrambled. She couldn't tell if it was because of the hearty shaking or because of what happened before it—the darkness, that awful darkness. The tiny space in the darkness, with nothing but Molly inside it. *Letmeoutletmeout.*

"What happened?" she gasped.

"You were calling for your father," Reggie said, grabbing her wrist and taking her pulse. His hand around her wrist reminded her of the black concrete box she'd just been in—it was like a vice—and there was something lumpy on his finger, something that was digging painfully into her skin. Her heart started beating even more quickly. "Hmm," Reggie said, releasing her wrist. There was a flash of something green as he moved his hand away. "This isn't good. Why were you calling for your father? Especially after what I told you before!"

The cold look in his eyes could have stopped an advancing army dead in its tracks. Frozen it solid.

"It was my fault," said Adam. "I, uh. . . ." Please, let me think of something, he thought, please please please! "Well," he finally said, "you know what an imagination I have, right? Sometimes I get carried away, and, well, I was describing those spiders to Molly and I guess I went into too much gory detail and, well, she had a panic at-tack, I guess, and started screaming for Dad."

A panic attack? Me? thought Molly. Now his im-agination really is running away from him—big time. Although, to be honest, he wasn't very far from the truth. Her heart was still pounding.

Reggie turned and looked at Adam in total disbelief.

"Really?" he said. "You *imagined* her into a panic attack? Well, kid, there's no question about it—you certainly do have some imagination."

"Yes," said Adam defiantly. "I do."

"This is absolutely the last straw," said Reggie. "There's been quite enough of this ridiculous imagin-ing going on around here. The next thing you know, you'll be making up stories about being stuck in small, dark places or something equally bizarre."

What? Molly stared at Reggie. How could he know about that? *Did* he know about it? Wasn't it her own private fear—one that she'd never mentioned to anybody, not even Adam, not even her parents?

"I'm sending you children outside," Reggie con-tinued, "right now. It's a beautiful sunny day out there. Go out and swim. Or lie on the dock. Whatever you want. I don't care, as long as it doesn't involve any more shouting and screaming. Just get out of here and leave me alone with your father. I'll keep an eye on him."

Glancing over her shoulder as Reggie dragged her out into the hallway, she could see Granddad peeking up from behind the desk, an anxious look on his face.

CHAPTER FIFTEEN
Facing the Ghosts

Reggie pushed them out the cottage door and shut it quietly behind them. For a moment they simply stood there on the porch, the sun shining, the wind light, the sky still a clear blue. The sun sparkled off the lake, and the water lapped gently onto the shore. Molly was struck by the normalcy of it all and once again felt that nothing that had been going on inside the cottage could be real. And yet, she knew that her definition of real had just changed forever.

"Now what?" she said, finally.

"Beats me," said Adam. "What happened to you, anyway?"

For a moment, Molly hesitated. She was always laughing at Adam when he scared himself with his silly daydreams. If she told him the truth, he'd tease her forever.

But he had to know. They both had to know everything—and they had to make sure Granddad knew, too. How else would they ever be able to solve the mystery and save Dad?

If, that is, he was still around to save. Now he was alone in the cottage with Reggie, sound asleep. Charlie was in there, too, but he wasn't likely to be of any real help. He was probably sound asleep, as well, and would probably jump out the window and head for the hills the minute he woke up and saw Reggie. Who knew what might happen while she and Adam both were stuck outside?

"I had a vision, too," she said. "I'll tell you about it, but first, we have to get back inside. We have to be near Dad, right? And we have to get back to Granddad and help him figure out the mystery. I'll tell you both the whole story when we're back inside."

She reached out for the doorknob, and began to turn it. It didn't budge. It was locked. She couldn't believe it! She shook it. "He's locked it!" Molly exclaimed. "He's actually locked us out of our own cottage! Who does he think he is, anyway?"

"A nurse," said Adam. "He thinks he's a nurse—and *maybe* he's only doing what he thinks he has to do to look after Dad."

"Maybe," said Molly. "But aren't you worried about him, I mean Reggie?"

"Yes," said Adam, "but we can't be sure, can we?"

"I think Granddad is right," said Molly. "There's something about him, something. . . ."

"Look at that," Adam said. He had edged over to the big living-room window, and was now kneeling beneath it, sticking his head up over the sill to look inside.

"He'll see you!" whispered Molly. "Get back here!"

"I don't think so," said Adam. "For one thing, his view of me is mostly hidden by Mom's rubber plant. And for another . . . well, take a look for yourself."

Molly joined him beneath the window and slowly, very slowly, raised her head.

Reggie was laid out full length on the sofa, his large feet dangling over the edge. He'd placed the knitting magazine over his face.

He couldn't possibly be asleep yet, but it was going to happen any minute now.

"What he really wanted was a nap himself," said Adam. "He probably wasn't thinking about Dad at all."

Molly wasn't so sure. "If he just wanted a nap, why didn't he go back to the Rosen's?"

"Well, he did say he would look after Dad. He probably wanted to stay close, just in case."

"Maybe," said Molly, still unconvinced. "But at least it buys us some time. It means we can go back and talk to Granddad."

Adam felt a shiver run up his spine. "I don't want to go back in there."

"I don't want to either," she said, "but what choice do we have?"

Sitting with his back against the wall of the cottage, Adam shrugged and stared out at the water. Maybe Granddad had thought of something. He hoped so. But to find out, he'd have to go back to where the boxes were. And horrible things happened when he went near the boxes. They happened to him and, as far as he could tell, they happened to Molly, too.

"It's those boxes," he said, shivering. "They scare me."

"Me too," said Molly. "But if those visions we had happened because of something supernatural," she said, "and I guess I have to admit there's a good chance that they did, then it probably means the boxes have the answers, otherwise why would these strange things be happening when we try to open them?" She sighed. "Come on, let's go in. Maybe Granddad has thought of something."

"Yeah, and how weird is that, anyways?" Adam said.

"You mean that we're getting advice from a ghost?" Adam nodded, then looked around.

"How will we get in?"

"The window!" Surely Reggie wasn't dumb enough to have left it open? She got up and headed toward it.

Reluctantly, Adam followed Molly around to the back of the cottage. Sure enough, the window was open—maybe Reggie wasn't such a threat after all. In a moment, Molly was pulling herself over the sill, with Adam right behind her.

"You're back," said Granddad. "Good! What happened to Reggie?"

"He's asleep on the sofa," Molly said. "And with any luck, he'll stay that way for a while."

"As long as we don't make too much noise," said Adam, whispering.

Molly went to the door and poked her head out into the hall. She could hear three sets of snores—two from the bedroom across the hall where Dad and Charlie were, and another from the living room.

"I don't think we'll need to whisper for a while," she said.

"Good," said Granddad. "Tell me what happened, Molly. What made you scream like that?"

She really didn't want to tell anybody. But she knew she had to.

"It was awful!" Molly exclaimed, tears burning at her eyes. "The walls closed in on me and I thought I'd be crushed. Or that I'd be trapped forever. It's the one thing that scares me," she said with a small shiver, "small spaces."

She waited for Adam to start laughing. But he didn't. He gave her a sympathetic look.

Granddad nodded, also sympathetically. "I saw it happen," he explained, "but I couldn't tell exactly what 'it' was. I simply saw blackness, blackness everywhere. And then a constricting feeling came over me, like a vice tightening around my heart. You know, I think I must have nearly died again!"

Me too, thought Molly.

"This is very serious," he said. "There has to be something in those papers, some clue as to what is causing all this and what caused my death. Someone or something does not want us to discover what that is."

"I'm not going near that box again!" Adam declared.

"Neither am I," Molly found herself saying, much to her surprise. But it was, she realized, the truth. The mere thought of getting any closer to the open box was giving her the willies.

"And I am unable to do so," Granddad said. "We seem to be at an impasse."

The three of them stood in silence, thinking.

Adam was pretty sure they were all thinking about the same thing: Dad. They were worried about Dad. It was only hours to his birthday now. And the only possible way of doing anything to stop a catastrophe was hidden in those boxes.

"Do we really need to look at those papers?" he asked. He knew he was whining but he couldn't help it. Why had he dropped those stupid ghost papers?

"Frankly," Granddad said, "I see no other option. Answers must be in there somewhere, or whatever is trying to keep us from discovering them wouldn't be resorting to these tricks. But if it makes you feel any better, I do think they are only tricks."

"What do you mean?" asked Molly.

"Well, there weren't really any spiders in there, correct?"

"It sure seemed like there were," Adam declared.

"But it was all just an illusion—it went away, and nothing was left behind. No spider bites, no webs, nothing."

"That's true," said Molly. "And what happened to me was the same. It was all in my mind." Although she certainly didn't like the idea that someone or something was capable of putting it there.

"So," said Granddad, "if one of you can bring yourself to look again, I must conclude it would be safe to do so. Although I do wish I could do it myself. I'd hate to ask anybody to go through something so horrid once, let alone a second time. And my own grandchildren, at that!" His voice quivered.

Well, thought Molly, if he would do it if he could, with his weak heart and all, then I'd better not say no.

However awful it is, thought Adam, it won't be anywhere as bad as losing Dad.

"I'll do it," they both said in unison—then looked at each other in surprise.

"It has to be done," Adam told Molly.

"I know," Molly told Adam.

"Let's do it together," they both said, in unison again.

"That would be wise," said Granddad. "Whatever this force is, it seems to depend on burrowing into your mind and finding your greatest fears. But you fear different things. Perhaps if you *both* pick up a paper at the same time, the force will be confused and produce less powerful effects."

"I sure hope so," said Molly.

"Me too," said Adam.

"And," added Granddad, "I seem to be able to see whatever each of you sees. So when something happens—if something happens—I'll call out and reassure you that it's only a trick of the mind. That ought to help, don't you think?"

They both nodded.

"Whatever appears," he continued, "your job is to ignore it. Just get those papers out of the box. Lay as many as possible out on the desk and then we'll go through them together." He paused. "What do you say?"

Molly looked at Adam. He was almost shaking with fear. She wasn't feeling so brave either. But what choice did they have? Soon, perhaps, their father would be the target of those powerful hallucinations and maybe they'd actually scare him to death. They had to act and act now.

"We can't let whatever this is get to Dad," Adam declared, although his teeth were chattering. He was imagining what the dark powers might have in store for him. Would he find himself covered in leeches, each one growing bigger and bigger, engorged with his blood? Would snakes slither out of the box, sliding all over him?

"Let's just get it over with," he almost shouted.

"Right now!" Molly added.

"Right now," Granddad agreed.

CHAPTER SIXTEEN
Ghost Attack

"Remember, listen to my voice," Granddad said, as Adam and Molly once again approached the open box. "I'll talk you through it."

Together they knelt, and Molly looked at Adam. "One," she said, "two, three!"

They reached in together and began pulling papers out. Quickly they shovelled as many as they could to the desk.

Adam heard a buzzing noise.

"I hear something," he said, alarmed.

"Don't stop!" said Granddad. "It's a wasp. I can see it. But don't stop! Remember, it isn't real!"

Adam looked into the box. It was still half full— and on top of the rest of the papers were about a dozen wasps.

"They aren't really there," Molly said, as she put her hands in and grabbed more papers. She pulled them out and dropped them onto the desk with the others. Adam did the same, closing his eyes so he wouldn't see the wasps.

But the buzzing was getting louder. Adam could feel them now—on his hands, his arms. He opened his eyes to see his hands covered in wasps.

"Ignore them!" his granddad shouted. "Drop the papers on my desk!"

Adam did, and then he screamed. "Ow! Ow! Ow!" He began to do a wild dance, nearly toppling the pile of boxes.

"What's happening?" Granddad called.

"They're stinging me!" Adam shrieked. It felt like he was being stabbed with sharp objects, sharp objects with poison on the tips. First a stab of pain and then a dreadful stinging that quickly began to burn on his hand, his wrists, his arms.

"They can't be stinging you, Adam!" Granddad insisted. "They aren't real. The pain isn't real, either. Tell yourself it isn't real! You can do it! I know you can."

Grandpa is right, thought Molly. "It isn't real, it isn't real, I know it isn't real," she said. But then she couldn't help herself. "Ouch!" she screamed. She pulled the last of the papers out. The pain was excruciating.

"*Wasps*! Wasps!" Reggie yelled, as he barrelled through the door. "Get out! Get out!"

As Molly and Adam shrieked and swatted at themselves and wasps filled the air, Reggie rushed over, put one of his thick arms around each of them, picked them up, and carried them through the door.

Once in the living room he tried to brush the wasps away with his huge hands, but they continued to swarm. There were wasps in their hair, on their clothes, on the couch.

"Where's the bug spray?" Reggie shouted.

"In—Ow!—In the—Ow!" said Molly.

"In the kitchen!" gasped Adam. "Ow! In the—Owww!"

"Under—Owww!—the sink!" screamed Molly.

As Reggie raced over and scrabbled through the junk under the sink Adam desperately tried to brush the wasps off of him and Molly, but there were too many.

Soon, Reggie was back, covering them both with bug spray. A lot of bug spray. Molly's hands went up to shield her eyes, then back down again to where wasps were still stinging. There was nothing to do but wait until it was over.

"There," Reggie said as the hissing of the spray finally fizzled out. "That should do it!"

He had emptied the entire can on them. Molly and Adam were completely coated in bug spray. But it had done the job. The cloud of wasps seemed to be gone.

"You both need antihistamines!" Reggie said as he raced out the door. "I'll get my bag and be right back."

Adam stood up and whirled in circles, trying to be sure there were no more wasps. Molly was doing the same. Suddenly, Molly swatted him on the back—hard.

"Ow!" he screamed.

"Sorry! There was one stuck on your shirt," she said. "What about me? Am I clear?" She twirled around in front of him.

He checked her over carefully. "Yep," he said. He didn't tell her she looked completely awful. She had bright-red bumps on her arms that glistened with a thick coat of bug spray.

I must look the same way, he thought, checking out his hands. Yup, just the same. Gooey and covered with red welts. And they were starting to swell up. And they hurt like crazy.

So did his leg. No, wait, that was Charlie, scratching his leg and wanting a pat. The commotion in the living room must have gotten his attention. "Go away, Charlie," he said. "Not now."

And surprisingly, Charlie *did* go away. As soon as Adam told him to, which was totally unlike Charlie, who always kept nudging at you and barking and had to be told at least four times. This time, however, he just slunk away under the chair.

"Here I am," said Reggie, back already with a black medical bag clutched in his hand.

He rummaged through the bag and brought out

a small tube of pills. "These'll do the job." He gave one pill to Molly and one to Adam, then dragged them both into the kitchen and poured two glasses of water.

"Take those," he ordered.

For a moment—a brief moment—Molly hesitated. Those pills might be anything. They might be poison.

But he *had* just saved them, hadn't he? And the pain in her hands was driving her wild. She knew from horrible past experience what happens after a wasp sting if you don't take an antihistamine. She never ever wanted to be that sore and itchy again. She'd just have to take the chance. She popped the pill into her mouth and gulped it down, and saw that Adam was doing the same.

"Good," said Reggie, as he grabbed their hands and forced them under the cold water.

Molly bit her lip. Man, it hurt. Adam was crying.

"That ought to do it," said Reggie. "Now show me where you've been stung."

Molly stuck out her bare arms.

"Not too terrible," said Reggie as he lifted her arms and turned them over, "considering. And you, kid?" He turned to Adam, who quickly stuck out his own arms so that Reggie wouldn't manhandle them.

Reggie manhandled him anyway, shaking his head side to side as he completed his inspection.

Adam had been stung on both hands.

"Let's just hope you're not allergic," Reggie said.

"We're not," Molly said. When she and Adam had been stung before, neither of them had gone into shock or anything like that.

Molly clenched her teeth and waited very impatiently for the pills to take effect.

"Anyway," said Reggie "you both seem to be all right. Where did all those wasps come from?"

"The boxes," Adam said. "In Molly's room."

"I'll take a look," said Reggie, as he headed off down the hall. "You two stay here," he said. "You need to rest."

A thought suddenly struck Molly. "You know what, Adam?" she said.

"What?" he said, squeezing his eyes shut to try to stop the tears.

"Those were real wasps!"

He gave her a nasty look. "You think?" he said. He waved his swelling hands in front of her.

"I know," said Molly. "but it's not just that—*he* could see them, too."

"He?"

"Reggie. And he's obviously not a ghost himself—not unless ghosts are made of solid concrete. Ooh, this hurts." She rapidly wiggled her arms back and forth, as if she were trying to shake the stings away.

Molly was right, Reggie had seen the wasps. Which meant—?

"I think I got them all," said Reggie as he came

back into the living room waving another can of bug spray. "Must have been a couple dozen at least. They must have made quite a nest in that box. Good thing I brought more spray from the Rosen's. Let me look at those stings again."

He took Adam's arm. Adam yelped. "Sorry," said Reggie, not sounding the least bit sorry. "Getting those pills into you so quickly was good, but you should take another dose in four hours."

Molly and Adam were both about to sink down on the couch when Reggie said, "Oh no you don't. You are both covered in bug spray. Go have a wash, each of you. It'll help the itch as well."

Neither had any fight left in them. Dutifully they tramped to the bathroom where Adam waited outside the door until Molly had showered off. Luckily she had thrown her shorts and top and underwear over the towel bar before going in for her swim and therefore she had clean clothes—she did not want to go back into her room yet. Adam went into his room, grabbed a pair of clean shorts and a t-shirt then followed Molly for his shower. She waited for him. They both dragged themselves back down the hall and sank down on the couch. Molly was feeling woozy from the pain and the shock, Adam was in a state of panic. Was this part of dealing with the dark forces? Or was this just normal lake stuff—the usual bugs and misery that came with being out here?

Things couldn't possibly get any worse.

"Wha's happenin'?" It was Dad, sounding even groggier than before. He was standing in the living room, wavering on his feet as if he was about to topple over.

In fact, it seemed, things could get worse. They just had. Adam sighed.

"I . . . I heard shum noish," said Dad. "Whus up?"

He seemed to be drunk or something. Those pills Reggie had given him, thought Molly. Could they really be good for him?

And if they weren't, what about the pills he'd given her and Adam?

Although, come to think of it, she was feeling much better now. Those pills, at least, had probably been real.

"Nothing, Tim," Reggie was telling Dad, "nothing's wrong. Everything's fine. Right, kids?" He gave them a look that told them they'd better agree or else.

"Uh, right," said Adam. Molly just nodded. She didn't know why Reggie was so determined to keep her dad out of the picture—or what to think about Reggie at all, now that he'd helped them with the wasp stings. Would he really have been so helpful if he was planning to do something awful to them? Was he just making them feel better so they'd be alive and healthy enough to really suffer when the time came? Was he as bad as he seemed? Or as good

CHAPTER SEVENTEEN
Ghosts in a Ring?

Molly watched as Adam went into his room next door, then opened the door of the Wonder Woman room just a little and very tentatively peeked in. Had Reggie sent her back here because he had something awful up his sleeve? Was it actually safe to go in?

There was no buzzing sound, no wasps as far as she could tell. But there was a nasty smell of bug spray. She stepped into the room, hurried over to the window and opened it wide as it would go.

And there was Adam, right outside.

"Shh," he said. "And get out of the way." He was already crawling over the sill.

"That didn't take you long," she said.

"There's no point in waiting. I mean, you know Reggie is going to come and check on us in a few minutes. Who knows how much time we've got?"

As they turned towards the desk, they could see Granddad staring anxiously at them. "Are you both all right? Dear me! Dear me!" he fussed.

"We're okay, Granddad," Adam assured him. "I mean, we'll survive. But those were no imaginary wasps!"

"Do you think they were, like, natural," Molly asked him, "or, you know, supernatural?" Was it possible that supernatural wasps could produce real stings? Or could ghosts grab you and give you real medicine? It was a horrible idea.

"I'm not sure," Granddad replied. "I suppose real wasps could have found their way into that box easily enough. Still, it's strange that it's the same box that gave us all that trouble in the first place. Bit too much of a coincidence, I think."

"I think so, too," said Molly, as she stared gloomily at her arm. The big red marks were fading as the antihistamine worked, but she could still feel the burning. "Let me see your hands, Adam."

He held them out. They looked worse than hers. Five stings, clearly visible—dark red, angry-looking circles.

"Do they still hurt?" she asked.

"What do you think?"

There was no doubt about it—the stings were all too real. But the more Molly looked around the room, the more she thought her Granddad was right. Maybe the wasps hadn't been *entirely* real. "Adam, how many wasps do you think there were in here?"

"I don't know . . . a couple of dozen?"

"And did you see Reggie come in with a garbage bag or the vacuum?"

"No."

"Then where are they? Where are the corpses?"

Molly was right. There were no dead wasps anywhere. They'd all just disappeared.

"Whatever or whoever this spirit is, it knows how to frighten people. What is your dad most afraid of?" Granddad asked Molly.

"Mom!" she laughed.

He smiled. "He has no fears?"

"None that we know of," Adam said. "Well, unless you count his plans not being followed." Dad did love his plans, and hated it when other people ignored them.

"I suppose we can't worry about what the spirit might come up with," Granddad said. "Instead, we need to figure out why all of this is happening, and as quickly as possible. Time is of the essence. Can you spread these papers out for me, Molly?"

The papers were still where they'd left them—some on the desk, and a few had fallen on the floor. Molly picked those up and then began to spread them out, covering the desk top. She still had a big bunch in her hand. They'd have to look at those after they finished with the first batch.

"You start there, Adam," said Granddad, pointing to his left. "Molly, you there." They came around the desk so that one was standing on either side of him, and they all started to read.

It was, Adam told himself, incredibly boring. Most of the papers were very old and very yellow, and some of them had crumbly edges where bits had broken off. Some were bills for dress shops and gas companies and milk deliveries. Some were legal papers, filled with "whereases" and "party-of-the-first-parts," and for Adam, totally meaningless. There was more, too: things that looked like graduation diplomas, old greeting cards, newspaper clippings, even some old photographs. These were mostly of unhappy-looking men in strange hats and unhappy-looking women in long dresses with their hair piled high on their heads.

How, thought Molly as she read, can we possibly figure out what we should be paying attention to? It could be anything. Maybe some business went bankrupt because somebody didn't pay this coal bill. Maybe somebody never got a thank you for this awful flowery birthday card and decided to take revenge. Who knows?

"Listen to this!" Granddad exclaimed. "It seems to be a page ripped from a diary or journal. It's dated August 18, 1889, and was written by your great-great-grandmother! These are papers I hadn't read yet when . . . well . . . when I died."

Adam and Molly both leaned over to get a closer look. The sheet of paper Granddad was holding was completely filled with tiny handwriting. Some of it was even written over the rest, going in the other direction, up and down instead of back and forth.

"It's impossible to read!" said Molly.

Adam nodded. The handwriting was almost as hard to read as his own—and his teachers were always telling him he had the worst handwriting they'd ever seen. Sometimes he couldn't even read it himself.

"It's quite clear to me," said Granddad.

"*We had to let Lucinda go today,*" he read. "*The ring has not yet been found. She begged for mercy, pleading her innocence, but she is the only one with access to my private boudoir, and thus to the ring. That ring may be worth the price of the entire house! I did feel badly letting her go. She has five young children, after all. Heaven knows how she will provide for them, since her no-good scoundrel of a husband did her a great favour and died of influenza last year. I encouraged her to give the ring back in exchange for clemency—but she continued to insist she knew nothing about it.*"

"I don't know if this is important," Granddad went on, "but it's the only thing that stands out—that seems out of the ordinary run of things, you know?

The rest of the papers are to do with land transactions and such."

"And gas bills," said Molly.

"Yes, and gas bills. But a missing ring—I wonder if there's anything more about it? Let's divide this up a little. Molly, put the papers we've already looked at aside, then spread out another batch for me. You and Adam can each take a pile and go through it as well.

"Remember," he said, "we're looking for anything to do with a ring."

"A ring," said Adam. "Hmmmm, I think I just—" He began to paw quickly through the papers he'd looked at and put aside. "Yes!" he said, grabbing a page and waving it in the air. "Here!"

"Let me see," said Molly, trying to take it from him.

"No," said Granddad. "Let me!" He reached for the page, but his hand went right through it.

"Oh, for heaven's sake," Adam said, placing it on the desk in front of his granddad. "Here."

Like the others, it was an old, yellowed sheet of paper. The words "Evaluation of a Ring for Sir Maurice Barnett, The Oaks, Toot Baldon, Oxfordshire" were underlined at the top, followed by a long paragraph:

A multi-stoned set ring with an 18 ct. yellow gold mount on 18 ct. white gold, with coronet peg settings. The ring is set with eight (8) round brilliant-

cut diamonds of top quality, calculated as weighing approx. 1 ct. each. The diamonds surround a marquis-cut emerald of 23 carats, known as the Evening Eye. It is of excellent quality except for one slight imperfection. The ring has a plain, polished, high-domed shank, rising and tapering to vertically split, semi-Chenier decorated shoulders. Hallmarked, Birmingham Town Mark, and Standard Mark and engraved on the interior with the words "To my dear Maude."

Value, £5000.00

I have examined the above scheduled item and in my opinion the value shown represents the value of such items on the basis noted, for the purpose declared on the date examined.

Signed: Ian Dunbar, jeweller to Her Majesty the Queen.

April 13, 1888.

"What a lot of gobblygook," said Molly.

"What does it mean?" asked Adam.

"It means," said Granddad, "that this family once owned a very valuable ring. A ring worth five thousand pounds in 1888 would be worth millions today!"

"Do you think it could be the one that was stolen?" asked Molly.

"It must be," said Granddad. "Our family was never rich enough to own two rings of this sort!

From the description, it appears that the emerald in it was unusual enough to have its own name. Worth stealing, I'd say. Worth getting fired over as well."

"Emerald?" said Molly, a strange look on her face. "That's green, right? It was a big, green emerald with lots of little white diamonds around it?"

"Yes," he said. "Why?"

"Because I think I've seen it. Today."

CHAPTER EIGHTEEN
A Ghost of a Nurse

Adam and Granddad both stared at Molly.

"You saw it today?" said Granddad.

"Where?" said Adam.

"Reggie had it on!" said Molly. "I noticed it when he was holding me around the wrist to take my pulse. I felt something digging into me, and I saw a gold band around one of his fingers. I guessed he was wearing a ring with the stone, or whatever it was that was digging into me, turned around to face the inside of his hand. And after he finished, I looked to see what it was, and I noticed something green. Look—it made a bruise on my wrist!" She held out her arm in front of Granddad. There was a black and blue mark on the back of Molly's wrist.

"Are you sure that's not just another wasp sting?" he asked.

"Positive. It wasn't there before he took my pulse."

"Wait a minute!" said Adam. "I think I remember that ring, too. It was right after we got stung, and he grabbed my arm, and—yes! It was a big green stone!"

"But," said Granddad, "let's think about this. It cannot be the same ring. That robbery happened more than a hundred years ago, and that nurse out there has nothing to do with our family."

"True," said Molly, slowly. "But Granddad, look at this!" She pointed to one of the pages spread out on the desk in front of him.

It was a clipping from a newspaper, at least as old and yellow as all the rest of the papers, with a note of some sort attached to it with a pin.

Granddad bent close to the paper to read it.

"Nurse Wins Coveted Royal Honour," its headline said, and there was a blurry picture of a woman in an old-fashioned nurse's uniform.

A woman with a huge square jaw beneath her down-turned lips.

A woman who looked a lot like Reggie.

"It's him!" said Adam, who was also reading the clipping, his head so close to his granddad's it was sometimes actually inside it. "Reggie! In a dress!"

"'Lyme Regis, 1903,'" Granddad read. "'Today a former citizen of our illustrious town was honoured

172

by the King in a ceremony at Buckingham Palace. For service to the country as a nursing sister during the recent South African War, the Royal Red Cross and the Queen's South Africa Medal were awarded to Miss Regina Crankshaft, known to her friends as—'"

"Reggie," said Adam. "That's *his* name. Reggie Crankshaft!"

"Except," said Molly, thinking of the huge slab of muscular humanity that she knew as Reggie, "he is not a woman!"

"He might be," said Adam. "After all, Molly, you're the one who keeps going on about how awful it is for women to have to deal with ridiculous body image stereotypes. She can't help it she doesn't look like a fashion model, right?"

"But," said Granddad, "it certainly doesn't explain how he can be alive more than one hundred years after this picture was taken." His brow wrinkled, and he seemed sunk in thought. "Unless he is somehow of the supernatural. . . ."

"A ghost?" said Adam.

"You can't photograph a ghost," Molly said. "Everyone knows that!"

"Not after he's become a ghost, at least," said Adam.

She took a closer look at the blurry black and white photo. It certainly looked like Reggie, all right. And he didn't look any less ridiculous in an old-fashioned nurse's uniform than he did in a loud pink and orange shirt. But. . . .

"Granddad," she said, "is there a magnifying glass in your desk?" Any real magnifying glass would have been removed from the drawer back in Oxford and sold along with the rest of Gram's furniture, but its ghost might still be in one of Granddad's drawers.

"Yes," he said, pointing to the centre drawer. "I keep one in there. But why?"

Molly slid the drawer open. "Can you take it out and take a closer look at the picture?"

He reached into the drawer and pulled out a magnifying glass. "What are we looking for?"

"Her hands," said Molly, pointing, "folded there on her knees. Look at her hands."

"Goodness me!" said Granddad, peering through the ghostly glass. "I can't believe it!"

"What is it?" said Adam, impatiently trying to look over Granddad's shoulder without actually entering it. "What can you see?"

"She's wearing a ring," he said. "A ring with a large stone. It might well be the same ring."

"Then . . . then . . . it is him!"

"It certainly seems that way," said Granddad. "Which means he must be the one—the one who stole the ring! The one who has been preying on our family for so long now!"

"But why?" said Adam. "What does Reggie Crankshaft have to do with our family? And what is he? A ghost, a spirit, the undead?"

"And if he is," added Molly. "How can he be so . . . well . . . so *here*. So real."

Adam shuddered. He decided not to try to imagine all the horrible possibilities.

"I don't know," said Granddad. "Perhaps whatever or whoever he is, he's merely trying to stop us from getting the ring back. It still legally belongs to us—to me when I was alive, and now, to your father. If we got it back now, your dad would be very rich." He stopped and thought again. "But how did he find us? And what does the ring have to do with my death and your dad's danger? Surely if he was merely trying to keep the ring to himself, he'd stay as far away from us as possible! There are too many unanswered questions."

Molly was perplexed. "Say he is a spirit," she said.

"Yes," said Granddad.

"Why would a spirit care if you or Dad were rich? It's not like a spirit would care about the money, so there has to be something else—another reason."

"Yes, there must be a reason that Reggie is preying on our family," Granddad agreed. "Perhaps that note might explain it."

"Note?"

"The one pinned to that clipping."

Molly had completely forgotten about the note. She turned the clipping over and began to read.

"What does it say?" said Adam impatiently.

"It's the same handwriting as in that diary," said Molly. She turned to Granddad. "Our great-great-grandmother?"

Granddad nodded.

"But I think I can make it out this time. It says, *'How wonderful for our old and devoted companion Reggie! I must write her and'*—this word is hard to make out—*'and congratulate her. She served the Barnett family well in our time of trial, when I was so severely ill in the weeks before Maurice's sudden death, and now she has served her country well, too.'*"

Molly and Adam looked at their grandfather, waiting for an explanation.

"So," said Granddad, "she worked for the family as a nurse. Maurice Barnett was my grandfather. Reggie must have been in the house when he died, just before his thirty-fifth birthday. And you know . . . ," he paused, a puzzled look on his face, "I'm almost certain *I've* seen her before, too. Not just in this newspaper photo, either—although I must have been looking at it just before. . . . Yes, I'm beginning to remember now! I *can* remember! I *was* looking at this photo, and then, I looked up from my desk and there she was— the same person, in the very same uniform! And then. . . then. . . ." He looked very confused. "That's all I can remember. Something bad happened. And she was there."

"And she—or he—is here again now!" said Adam.

"We have to do something," said Molly. "Right away. We have to protect Dad from—from who? Or is it, is it . . . what?"

"Children!" a deep voice boomed. It was Reggie, standing once more in the doorway.

CHAPTER NINETEEN
Whose Ghost There?

As Reggie advanced into the room, Molly and Adam both stared at him, so frightened they couldn't move, couldn't think.

It was not a large room. In a few more steps he would reach them, and then——.

"No!" It was Granddad, shouting! He was in full view behind the desk, his long hair flying wildly as he violently shook his head back and forth. He pointed his arm at Reggie. "You leave my grandchildren alone! You may have killed me, Miss Reggie Crankshaft——or whoever you are——but you won't kill them! Not if I can help it!"

Reggie stopped dead in his tracks. He stared over Adam and Molly's head, straight at the desk. For a moment, he seemed bewildered, uncertain, his eyes nearly popping out of his head. "Is it——? Are you——?"

A look of absolute terror crept over his face, and then a most surprising thing happened—a thing neither Molly nor Adam could have imagined. Reggie Crankshaft began to scream.

It was a huge, loud, surprisingly high-pitched scream, and it went on for some time. For Molly and Adam, it felt like almost forever.

And then, Reggie fainted.

As his hulking body hit the floor, the entire cottage shook.

For a moment, Adam just stared. He was waiting for Reggie to pop right back up and come after him and Molly again, or turn into a wisp of flame and fly up through the roof, or disintegrate into a pile of dust, or just plain disappear from view. Reggie was a ghost, wasn't he? Wasn't that what ghosts did?

But what happened next was the most surprising thing of all.

Nothing. Nothing at all.

The body just lay there on the floor, and they just stood there staring at it.

Finally Molly leapt into action. "Quick, Adam," she said, bending over Reggie's head. "He's breathing. He's still alive—or, I guess, still pretending to be alive—and he's obviously figured out we're on to him. We're going to have to tie him up or something. I think there are a couple of old skipping ropes at the back of the closet—I'll get them! You find something to make a gag out of. We don't want him to call out again and wake up Dad."

Adam nodded, and forced himself to move. Tying up a ghost—ridiculous! It made no sense, no sense at all. Which kind of made him happy—the world was becoming more like his daydreams with every passing minute! And anyway, Molly was right. Reggie did need to be tied up. For a ghost, he sure did occupy real space. Occupied a lot of it. Occupied it danger- ously. Skipping ropes and gags were a good idea.

In a surprisingly short time, they had Reggie's hands tied up in one skipping rope and his feet in another. A gag made of a torn-up pillow case was stuffed in his mouth and tied around his head.

"Good work," said Granddad. "That'll hold him while we think of what to do next. Because—"

"Reggie? Kids?" It was Dad's voice. "Are you in there?"

And before anyone could think of anything to do to stop him, Dad was in the room.

No! thought Molly! He can't come in here now! He'll be furious with us for this!

Or at least, she told herself, he'll be furious if he survives the shock of seeing it. Which he probably won't.

They had done the very thing they were trying to prevent.

Although Dad was certainly looking a lot better

than he had just a while before. He was back up on his feet again, and, it seemed, walking on his bad ankle without too much pain. And his voice wasn't slurred any more—the effects of the drugs Reggie had given him seemed to have worn off. He actually appeared quite well, and very chipper.

"I've started some steaks," he said, "and—" He stopped and stared at the bound and gagged body of Reggie, lying on the floor at his feet. He looked at Molly and Adam in complete bewilderment. "What's going on in here?"

"Well, uh, we—" said Molly.

"It just—" said Adam at the same time. Then they both stopped and waited for the other to continue. Adam was sure that what Molly had to say was better than anything he could come up with. Molly felt exactly the same way.

But neither said anything.

"He was—" said Molly.

"We were—" said Adam.

Then they both stopped again.

"Have you two lost your minds?" their Dad exclaimed.

At least, thought Adam, he's too busy concentrating on Reggie to notice his dead father!

Tim bent down over Reggie and began to untie the skipping ropes.

"Dad," said Adam, "you can't do that!"

"I certainly can. What on earth . . . ?" He wasn't having much success in untying the knots. "Untie him!" he ordered. "He's unconscious! I'll have to call 911."

Neither of them moved. "All right. I can't even imagine what's going on in here, but you two have just. . . . I'm going to get a knife to cut him loose."

He got up and hurried out the door.

"We have to tell Dad about Reggie," Molly said, "before Reggie wakes up and before Dad unties him."

"But—" Adam interrupted.

"We have to risk it, because if we don't, Reggie will kill him for sure."

"What? What are you . . ." It was Dad. He was shouting and it sounded to Molly as if he was still in the hallway.

And then she heard him scream—a distorted, weirdly strangled sound.

And now Dad was in the doorway again, but this time, he was backing slowly into the room as he stared at something out there in the hall.

He screamed again.

Molly could see why. As Dad backed further into the room and cowered against the pile of boxes in front of the desk, Molly and Adam could see what he was staring at.

A person with a crazy, demented look, a triumphant grin on her face. A person holding the sharpest of the kitchen knives over her head as she advanced into the room, advanced towards Dad.

Mom.

It was Molly and Adam's mother! Her face was distorted, it didn't look anything like Mom usually did. But it was her, all right—she was still wearing the same suit she'd had on that morning when she said goodbye to them in the city. Which now seemed ages and ages ago. It was Mom. And it looked like she was trying to kill their dad!

CHAPTER TWENTY
Contract with a Ghost

"**M**om! Stop it right now!" Adam exclaimed. "This isn't funny!"

"I'm not your mom!" It certainly didn't sound anything like Mom, even though the words were coming from Mom's mouth. The voice was high and shrill and had an accent that sounded like the man in the butcher shop that Gram went to in England.

She moved the knife swiftly through the air. "Come closer. I'll prove it to you."

"How?" Molly asked, her voice trembling. She grabbed Adam's hand.

"Your mother couldn't chop off your fingers and your toes, but I can! Which one of you wants to go first?" She looked deadly serious.

"Molly! Adam! The window! Run and get help!" Dad yelled.

"Lucinda!" It was Granddad's voice. "Is that you?"

Oh, no, thought Molly. As if Mom turning into a maniac isn't enough, now Dad is going to see his own dead father. As her dad turned toward the desk to see where the voice was coming from, he froze. Now he was staring even more intensely at Granddad than he had been staring at his wife—who was staring at Granddad also.

"Dad?" To Molly, the voice coming from her dad's mouth had a strangled sound. Was his heart giving out?

"Mr. Barnett?" said the strange voice coming out of their mom's mouth. "Ernest Barnett of Oxford?"

"Is that you?" Dad and the strange voice both spoke together.

And then, Dad fell to the floor.

It had finally been too much. He had fainted. Or was it even worse?

"Hold it right there," said the voice coming from Mom as Molly bent to take care of her father. "Stay where you are." She waved the knife toward them, then turned back to Granddad.

"I thought you were dead," the voice said. "I seem to remember you dying."

"Yes, and I remember you now, too," said Granddad. "Of course, you looked quite different then—it's that Yorkshire accent of yours that reminded me. You were there in my study! Reggie was there, too. I thought she had been there alone, but no." He paused. "You didn't have a knife that time—it was rats, I believe. Yes rats, I remember seeing rats. Rats everywhere. I've always had a phobia about rats. They were crawling over me, biting me, going for my eyes, and then . . . a terrible crushing pain in my chest, and all went black."

"As well it should have," said the voice. "You were just about to turn thirty-five, like all the others. Like me. I was just about to turn thirty-five when I died—still young. I died in utter poverty after I was fired for stealing a ring I never stole. Falsely accused, falsely dismissed! Because of the Barnett family I perished of consumption before my time and left five young children behind to face the world on their own, without parents, without prospects. I vowed to avenge myself by killing all the male Barnetts at the same age that I had died. And the women? I decided to leave them behind to raise the children alone, the way I'd had to. And the plan worked! I have triumphed each time! Except, you are here! Why aren't you dead?" She approached the desk, waving the knife menacingly in Granddad's direction. She stepped over their dad, still unconscious (or worse) on the floor. She leaned right over the desk. She raised the knife over her head. She plunged it down, down, down into Granddad's chest.

And of course, Granddad was gone again.

But not for long.

"No need for that, dear," he said, smiling at her

as he reappeared. "I'm dead already. Quite completely dead. Just a spirit, like you."

For a moment she remained suspended over the desk, panting heavily. Then she stepped back.

"And thank heavens for that. But this one," she waved the knife in Dad's direction, "I believe *he's* still alive!

Adam was trying to figure out if there was some way he could sneak up behind Mom or whoever or whatever it was that looked so much like Mom.

"But not for long," the voice added. "His time has come. And I'm tired now, very tired. There's no need for more silly games—no rats this time. No spiders or wasps or small dark spaces. You know who I am now, and what I intend to do."

So, thought Molly, she'd done all of that, too. Lucinda. The maid her great-great-grandmother had dismissed. The woman who's spirit was now in her mother's body!

"No," the voice continued. "I think I'll just use this."

And she raised the knife over her head, and prepared to plunge it down into Dad.

"No!" Adam shouted as he tried to grab her arm.

"Don't do it," Molly screamed, also reaching for the knife.

"No!" shouted Granddad. "Wait!"

She stopped, the knife still suspended over their dad.

"Why should I?" said the voice.

"Because I can help you," Granddad said.

"Help me?"

"Yes. I can clear your name! Prove you were innocent."

"I *am* innocent," the voice said. "But no one believed it—not the magistrate, not my neighbours, not even my own brothers and sisters. I will be stuck with this awful blot on my good name forever!"

"But you don't need to be," said Granddad. "I will work to restore your reputation. I and my grandchildren here"—he waved toward Molly and Adam—"will work together. We can research on two planes of existence at once! We will find the real thief who stole that ring—I'm sure we can do it! I have good reason to believe we can. And then, your name will be cleared! Your spirit will be free of this torment, free to move on."

"Cleared," the voice said quietly, the hand holding the knife dropping to her side. "Free."

"Yes, free! Free to join your loved ones who have moved on!"

She turned back to Granddad, and the knife fell from her hand.

"I agree," she said, her voice much less shrill. "I will give you until your son's next birthday. But that is all. If you haven't discovered the truth by then, I'll be back. I'll be back, and he'll face a death more horrible than any of the rest of you! I promise he will!"

And then, Mom's body slumped to the floor.

The spirit was gone.

CHAPTER TWENTY-ONE
Ghosts Gone

Looking around the Wonder Woman room, Molly couldn't believe what she was seeing. Bodies. There were bodies everywhere. It reminded Molly of the end of that *Hamlet* movie Dad had made her and Adam watch last winter. Dad loved Shakespeare.

Or at least he used to love it. Because now he was one of the bodies. And so was Mom. And so, Molly, could see, was Adam. What had happened to Adam?

In *Hamlet*, the bodies were all dead. Surely at least some members of Molly's family were still alive? Surely she couldn't be the only one left?

Suddenly, a bolt of pure energy zoomed through the door and leapt up onto Molly. Charlie! So she wasn't the only one left after all. He was licking her knees and squeaking and acting as if she was the best thing that had ever happened to him. Whatever had been bothering Charlie before sure wasn't bothering him now. Had it been the spirit?

"Stop it, Charlie," she said, pushing him down. "Not now."

Charlie rushed over to Mom and began to lick her face.

"Ohhhh!" said Mom. "Stop it, Charlie."

"Mom!" Molly cried.

"Molly?" Mom pushed the dog away and slowly sat up, looking very confused. "What are you doing here? Where am I?"

"You're okay!" Molly went over and got down on her knees and hugged her mother. "You're at the cottage! In the Wonder Woman room!"

"But . . . but I can't be. I was in my office at the hospital. I had just sent in my report." Bewildered, she looked around. "Except . . . except I'm not in the hospital. I'm. . . . It *is* the Wonder Woman room. I don't understand."

She's not the only one, thought Molly. How can I explain it all to her?

But before she could even begin to try, she heard another voice.

"Lily?" It was Dad, calling Mom's name. He was alive! Molly had been sure he'd been frightened to death. But he hadn't been. "Stop that, Charlie. What are you doing here, Lily?" he said to Mom. "I thought you were still in the city!"

"I thought so too," Mom said, looking around the room in that dazed way again. "Except I'm not. I'm here. Why am I here?"

"Hey, Mom," said Adam. He was alive, too! "Ugh. You have very bad breath, Charlie. It's disgusting."

The last thing Adam remembered was the spirit— or whatever it was inside of Mom—lifting the knife over Dad. So he must have fainted again. And no wonder—seeing your Mom about to kill your Dad was not a pleasant sight. But apparently, it hadn't happened. Dad seemed to be fine—and Mom was back to being Mom.

Except for being confused about what had happened to bring her to the lake. She turned to Dad. "What are you doing down here on the floor?"

"I'm not really sure," he said. "I remember I was feeling much better and I decided to cook up some steaks for dinner and I sent Reggie—the nurse, you know, from the Rosen's? I sent him in to tell the kids it was soon time to eat, and," suddenly his face changed. "Reggie! The kids had him all tied up with skipping ropes."

Dad began to climb to his feet. "We have to untie him! And then, you two are going to have some explaining to do. Where is he?" said Dad. "What have you done with him now?"

Molly looked over to the place near the door where they'd tied Reggie up.

Reggie wasn't there.

Dad bent down and picked up the skipping ropes and the gag. The ropes were still tied together and knotted.

Impossible, thought Adam. Molly tied those ropes really tight—so tight Dad couldn't undo them. That's why Dad was going for the knife. And he himself had knotted the gag the way he'd learned on the Secret-Agents-R-Us website. It was impossible to untie, at least according to the website. But Reggie was gone, no question about it.

"You tied him up?" Mom was on her feet now, too. "A guest in the house? A nurse helping your father— helping him, I recall, after you made your father fall in the first place, Molly."

"But I didn't, it was—"

"You two certainly do have a lot of explaining to do. Especially when your father is in so much—." She stopped and turned back to Dad. "Tim? All this excitement . . . your heart . . . are you sure you're okay?"

"I'm fine," Dad said, reaching over to Charlie and petting him as he talked. "I don't know why you're so worried."

"I thought. . . . Well. . . . It's just. . . ." She suddenly stopped. Molly could see that she didn't want to tell him what she'd really been thinking. "Well, you know how I worry."

"There's nothing to worry about," he said, smiling.

He turned to Molly and Adam, a strange look on his face. "I must have just imagined all that business about Reggie being tied up. Right, kidlets?"

"What are you talking about, Dad?" said Adam. "I mean, you can see the ropes right over there, and——"

"Dad's right, Adam," Molly interrupted. "He was sort of in a daze from the painkillers Reggie gave him, right? And he heard us playing that game—you know, the one where we pretend to tie someone up? Right, Adam? And he imagined it was real."

For some reason, Dad wanted Mom to think the whole thing had never happened. Maybe just to stop her worrying? Whatever. To Molly, it seemed like a good idea to play along. It was certainly better than dealing with the punishment. And poor Mom had enough on her mind. They could sort it all out later.

"Of course," said Dad, "that must be it. You worry too much, Lily. Coming all the way out here from the city for no reason at all!"

"But I didn't," said Mom, "really, I. . . ." She paused, a bewildered look on her face. "But I guess I must have, because why else——?" She sighed. "You're right, Tim."

"Of course I am! Nothing really happened, and everything is okay."

"Of course," said Mom. "Perfectly okay."

Adam couldn't believe it. Had his parents gone totally nuts? All these strange things were happening, and they were acting as if it was just an ordinary day at the lake.

And Molly was going along with them, too. Well, maybe it was better than thinking about what really had happened. *That* was enough to drive everyone completely crazy.

And besides, it was still a few hours until midnight, and Dad's birthday. Maybe Mom just wanted to stop Dad from being excited. Maybe Dad was just trying to stop *himself* from being excited.

"Oh!" said Dad. "I completely forgot! The steaks. They'll certainly be cooked by now. Kids, go wash up. We're going to eat."

"Excellent idea," said Mom.

"Great," said Molly.

Well, thought Adam, maybe they were right.

"Great," he said.

CHAPTER TWENTY-TWO
After the Ghost

And they did eat. They cleaned up and had dinner. And then they washed all the dishes. And then they played Cheat. And through it all, Charlie kept running from one of them to another, demanding attention and reassurance. *He* certainly hadn't forgotten anything.

But he seemed to be the only one. No one else did a single thing or said a single word to suggest they had any memory of the strange things that had just happened. It was as if those things had never happened at all.

Well, thought Molly, I guess we all have good reasons for avoiding the subject. For even thinking about it. It was way better to pretend that they were a perfectly normal family without ghosts in their lives. In fact, pretending felt pretty good.

Finally, after their fourth game of Cheat, Mom

looked at her watch. "I think we can all go to bed now," she said.

Molly looked at her watch, too. It was two minutes past midnight.

It was Dad's birthday!

No wonder Mom had been pretending to be so calm and had let them stay up so late and had kept them all together. Dad was fine. He was still alive! Dad was the first male Barnett in centuries to actually make it to his thirty-fifth birthday.

Lucinda was keeping her end of the bargain.

Now they just had to keep theirs.

"Happy birthday, Tim," said Mom, giving him a huge hug and a kiss.

As hugs and kisses were shared around the table, Adam couldn't help but notice that his mom and dad no longer seemed to be pretending. They really did seem to have completely forgotten about Mom suddenly showing up, and about Reggie, and about Granddad. Would they ever remember—or had the spirits done something to make sure that that wouldn't happen? And if they did remember, what would he and Molly tell them? They were going to have to get their stories straight, for sure.

After saying goodnight to Mom and Dad, and wishing Dad happy birthday one last time, Adam followed Molly into her room. And there was Granddad behind his desk.

"Where were you while Mom and Dad were waking up?" Molly said. "Were you hiding so you wouldn't upset Dad anymore?"

"Quite right," Granddad said. "Timmie and your mom had enough to worry about without me sticking my oar in." Molly told Granddad the good news— that it was past midnight and dad was fine.

"He made it!" said Granddad with a sigh of relief.

"Thanks to you and that deal you made with the ghost," said Molly. "How did you know it wasn't Mom? How did you know *who* it was?"

"When I saw her with that knife, I deduced it must be another case of spirit possession. A number have been reported, as I told you earlier. And since we had already postulated that this particular spirit had inhabited you, Molly, when the others heard you shouting before your father fell, it seemed logical that it might do so again."

"So," said Adam, "it was the same spirit in Mom that was in Molly before?"

"It seems most likely," said Granddad. "And after we'd learned about that maid Lucinda who was fired, I thought there might be a good chance it was her. She was the only person I ever found in all my research with a serious reason to have a grudge against the Barnetts. That's why I called her name. When she answered to it, I knew I was right."

"But," said Adam, "how could she possess Mom

like that? I mean, for her to get Mom all the way from the city and out here to the lake, she must have been in control of Mom for hours and hours."

"And," added Molly, "she came from a time before cars were invented, didn't she?"

Granddad nodded.

"So how could she drive Mom's car?"

"It's truly mysterious," said Granddad. "I just don't know."

"Maybe," said Adam, "maybe she could read Mom's thoughts while she was in there, and figure out how to drive from them." The mere thought made him shiver. Having someone control you from inside your head was bad enough. Them being able to read your thoughts was just plain creepy.

"And anyway," said Molly, "if she just wanted to use that knife on Dad, there are lots of people out here at the lake she could have possessed. Why go to the trouble of bringing Mom all the way out from the city?"

"I think you know the answer to that one, Molly," said Granddad. "To begin with, she wanted to *scare* your dad to death, like she did to me with the rats. The only reason she decided to use the knife was because she was tired. And before, when I asked you what your father was most scared of, what did you say?"

"I said it was Mom. But I was just joking!" Still, though,

thought Molly, it was actually sort of true. Mom was the only one who could get Dad to do things he didn't want to do. He was kind of scared of making her upset with him, in a good sort of way.

And seeing someone you love, someone you know loves you, coming at you with hatred in her eyes—that must be the scariest thing of all.

"At any rate," said Granddad, "I was able to make that deal with her. Your father is safe. For now."

"Although he's acting pretty strangely," said Adam, "and so is Mom." They told their granddad about how their parents seemed to have completely forgotten everything that had happened, how they hardly seemed to remember Reggie even.

"That is certainly strange," said Granddad, "but not necessarily a bad thing. There's no point in dragging them into all of this anymore than necessary, if we can possibly help it. Is there?"

Adam and Molly both shook their heads.

"Meanwhile," added Granddad, "we need only figure out who really did steal that ring. And with Reggie all tied up beyond those boxes and ready to explain it, we'll know that in jig time."

Oops.

"He's gone, Granddad," said Adam. "Gone, and taken the ring with him."

"What?" Granddad looked confused. "But I thought he was lying right over there."

"Yes," said Molly, "he was. And I think he was still there after Lucinda left. I'm almost positive I saw him after that. But maybe when I was trying to wake up Mom and Dad and Adam he slipped away?"

"Anyway," added Adam, "he managed to get out of the ropes without untying them."

"Really?" said Granddad. "Well, we did think he might be a spirit. And a spirit would certainly be capable of doing that."

"On the other hand," said Molly, "we know now that it wasn't Reggie who was after Dad. He wasn't the one who cooked up those visions to keep us from looking at the papers—the one who was trying to scare Dad to death."

"That's true," said Granddad.

"So maybe," Molly went on, "he wasn't a spirit at all. I mean, he could be a living grandson or great-grandson of that nurse in the picture, couldn't he? A real person with a strong family resemblance, like you and Dad and Adam? And maybe Reggie is a family name or something."

"I hadn't thought of that," said Granddad, sounding embarrassed. "You could be right, Molly. I am far too willing to believe in spirits simply because I want them to exist. I should have thought of that myself."

"I should have, too," said Molly. She was supposed to be the logical one.

"But," said Adam, "if he wasn't a ghost, then why

was he here? And where did he go? And how did he get free from those ropes?"

"He might really be just a nurse on vacation, staying next door at the Rosen's," said Molly. "He might have gone back there. If I were him, I'd be wanting to get away from us and this place as quickly as I could." She looked around the room—it certainly was a terrible mess. And so was the rest of their lives. Ghosts, missing rings, papers sloppily piled up everywhere. Something had to be done to tidy it all up. Soon.

"You have a point there," said Adam.

"Or maybe," said Granddad, "he's a ghost hunter, that nurse—a medium, attracted by the presence of the spirit. Perhaps he works on the side of good!"

"Or maybe," said Adam, "he actually *is* a spirit, but he came here to try to protect you from Lucinda. After all, he did have that ring—the one Lucinda was accused of stealing. He must be mixed up in all this somehow."

"Yes," said Granddad. "Maybe I have more friends on this side than I realized. Maybe it's to do with me, somehow. Maybe Dora sent him to look after me!"

"Which might explain something else," said Adam.

"What?" said Molly and Granddad together.

"Why Granddad is still here. I mean, he has his proof that ghosts exist. He *is* his proof that ghosts exist. So why is he still here? Shouldn't he be gone now?"

"No," said Molly, "not if he's here to protect Dad. We need to clear Lucinda's name before he's completely safe. And another thing," Molly added, perplexed. "Lucinda could be here and in the city almost at the same time. It looks like she can probably be anywhere she wants to go. And Reggie, well, if he's a ghost, he can get around, too. So why is Granddad attached to that desk?"

"What if it has something to do with the family curse," said Adam. "With all those papers. Maybe there is still something else in them he has to find. And hey, maybe that something has to do with Reggie. Maybe Reggie showed up here because he has some sort of unfinished business with Granddad. He *does* have the ring, right?"

"Maybe," said Molly. "But whatever it is, we're going to have to find him. Human or spirit makes no matter. Reggie has the ring, all right, and the key to the mystery. Finding him is the only way we can protect Dad."

"Then that's what we'll have to do," said Adam.

"Your dad is a lucky man to have two plucky kids like you," said Granddad.

Molly blushed. Adam blushed, too. And they tried not to think too hard about what was still in store for them. At least, right now, Dad was safe and so were they.

They looked at each other.

"Rosen's house?" said Molly.

"Lead the way!" said Adam.

Don't miss

The Curse of the Evening Eye,

Book II of the Ghosthunters series,
coming in Spring 2009
Turn the page for a sneak peek!

Prologue

The marked one.

The one she wanted.

She stood over him and smiled. "And you, sir? Can I get you something?" The voice coming out of the mouth she controlled was impossibly sweet, outrageously kind—as sweet as the head it belonged to, the head she now possessed. The head was full of sugar and spice and everything nice. She hated it.

On the bright side, she wouldn't need the head for long, or the body it was attached to. This newfangled flying machine might be horrifying—she could not understand why something that must weigh so many, many tons did not simply crash to the ground and fall into a million pieces, killing everyone on board (it would serve them right for presuming to defy the laws of nature)—but at least the machine moved quickly. They'd reach their destination in just a few more hours now. Soon she could leave the flying machine along with that cursed family in row 12 and find a better head to occupy—one that wouldn't suffocate her with its depressing sea of sweet niceness.

The marked one hadn't answered her.

"Excuse me, sir," she repeated. "A drink?"

"No, thanks," he said, a frown on his forehead, not even looking up from the papers that absorbed him. But the two unmannerly youngsters beside him were making demands even before she spoke to them.

"I'll have a tomato juice," the girl said. "No ice."

"And I'll have a Pepsi," the boy added, "with lots of ice."

"And a slice of lemon if you have it," the girl continued. "And also a glass of water. I am soooo dry."

"Yes, miss," she said. "Yes, sir." As she allowed the nice woman's hands to prepare the drinks and tried to control the anger rising within her, she reminded herself that she was bound to have her revenge some day.

First the father, of course. First things first. And then, in only another twenty-five or so years, the boy. He could have his ice now—she scooped a number of cubes into his glass—but she'd soon have her revenge.

A small fragment of a triumphant laugh burst from the mouth she had taken over, making the boy and girl give her a strange look. She made the mouth smile at them as she poured the ugly brown liquid over the ice.

The smile did its job. The girl looked away and turned to her father. "Are you sure you're okay?" she asked.

"Molly," he replied impatiently, "I'm fine. I've told you I'm fine about a hundred times already. You and

Adam saw me take my pills before I got on the plane. And anyway, it's been a smooth flight. I wouldn't even notice I was up in the air at all if you didn't keep constantly reminding me of it."

"I told you, Molly," the boy said, taking the glass from the nice woman's hands without even a word of thanks. "If you'd just stop bugging him about it, he could relax. How would you like it if you were scared of flying and someone kept reminding you of it, right in the middle of a flight?"

"I am not scared, Adam," the marked one said. "I just get a little anxious."

"A little?" the boy said. "But you——" The unmannerly child seemed to suddenly realize he was making things worse. He stopped in mid-sentence and quickly swallowed a large amount of the disgusting brown liquid.

"A little," the marked one insisted. "Just a little. It's the turbulence that gets me."

She could tell he wasn't telling the truth. His voice was strained, and there were beads of perspiration on his forehead. The marked one was frightened of the flying machine. Very frightened. He was especially frightened of something called turbulence.

Turbulence. She knew what that was. The men up front driving the infernal machine had been talking about it when she brought them their drinks earlier—talking about how they weren't expecting any on this trip. Turbulence meant hitting a kind of bump in the air that made the flying machine suddenly go down and then up again. It meant drinks flying and people screaming. It meant giving the marked one a very large scare—perhaps even a lethal scare.

Turbulence. What an excellent idea!

Pulling the cart behind her, she backed her way down the aisle toward the driver's room. A small nudge of his mind—a vision of the flying machine in flames, perhaps. That ought to do it.

Chapter One

I can't believe it! Molly thought.

She peered out the airplane window. *I'm actually sitting here with Dad and Adam, flying to Palm Springs! Palm Springs! How sweet is that?*

Adam was thinking the exact same thing. *Unreal!* he thought. *We did it. I can't believe we talked Mom and Dad into it.*

He slid a glance over at his dad who was sitting in the aisle seat, working away. Then her turned to Molly, who had a little grin on her face as she gazed out the window. He leaned over her to see if there was anything interesting out there.

She gave him a small shove and looked at her watch. "I have fifteen more minutes by the window," she said. "So stop hovering all over me."

Brothers! Still, Molly had to admit she was very glad he was along—although right now he was probably imagining that a UFO was going to swoop down out of the sky or space or somewhere and grab the plane and they would disappear mysteriously and never be heard from again. But Adam's imagination had turned out to be very useful a few months ago, during the terrifying events at the cottage. Every time Molly thought about it, she shuddered. It seemed like yesterday. It was all still so vivid.

They had raced over to the Rosen's cottage right after all those strange things had happened, hoping to find Reggie and figure out who he was. But if he'd been there at all, he'd already gone. The next day, they'd called the Rosens and asked about him. Apparently, a person called Reggie really had rented the cottage. So Reggie was, at least, real—not a ghost. Or so they thought. After all, the one ghost they were sure they were dealing with had figured out how to drive a car, so why shouldn't another one arrange to rent a cottage?

And then . . . then they'd made that *other* discovery—the one that was so scary they knew they couldn't let Dad go to Palm Springs alone. The one they hadn't told him about yet, because they didn't want to worry him. The one that had made them wheedle themselves onto the trip with Dad so they could watch him and keep him safe. Molly wondered when would be a good time to tell him. She sighed. Never. But they'd have to, and soon.

The plane gave a little jump. Molly felt it in her

stomach. She loved the feeling. She knew that air pockets were perfectly safe, but she also knew that Dad didn't know that. Well, he knew it, but somehow, he just didn't believe it. Adam threw her a worried look. "What was that?"

"Nothing," Molly answered. "Just a little turbulence. Is your seat belt buckled?"

Adam checked. It was. He looked at his dad, who had clutched the armrest and was still clutching it. "Hey Dad, want to play cards?"

"Sure," Tim answered. Not a good sign. He'd wanted to work but now, obviously, he needed to be distracted.

Adam watched as his Dad checked their seat belts, checked his, and then called the stewardess over. The stewardess with the fake smile. She was just a little creepy, Adam thought, like a Stepford wife or something. So nice it hurt.

"Yes, sir?" she smiled.

"Is everything all right?" Dad asked.

"Why, just fine sir," she said. "I hope." Her smile grew even wider.

"What? What?" said Dad, turning white. "You hope?"

"Oh, no sir! I didn't say that." She smiled again and moved away.

But she *had* said it. Adam had heard her. What was that about?

And then the plane bumped again. And again. And again. And then it lurched sideways. That gave even Molly pause. Up and down she had experienced, when they all flew to Minneapolis together through a thunderstorm, but sideways? A baby started to cry. Molly's ears popped. Adam grabbed his drink just before it flew off the tray but Molly didn't grab hers in time and it keeled over right onto Adam's leg.

"Oh, no! Great! Tomato juice all over me! Couldn't you have just had the water?"

"Adam!" Dad said. "It'll wash off. We have more important—"

Dad's words were cut off by the sudden plunging of the plane, the lights going off, and everyone screaming at once. Molly grabbed for Adam, Adam grabbed for Dad and they all held onto each other for dear life. Adam was just as terrified that his Dad would have a heart attack and die from fear as he was that the plane was about to crash. But much to his surprise he heard his Dad's voice, quiet and reassuring. "It's okay, kids. We're all going to be fine. Don't be afraid."

And then the stewardess was standing over them, and if looks could kill, then the one she wore on her face was lethal. She was scowling at Dad as if he was some sort of monster. Then the lights went on, her fake sweet smile came back, the plane levelled off, and everyone started to clap.

The pilot got on the air and assured the passengers that all was well—they had been trying to avoid something, something. . . . He sounded a little weirded out about it, Adam thought. But Adam really didn't care. They were all fine.

"That was odd," Dad said. "I was so worried about making sure you two weren't frightened that I wasn't scared a bit. Hah! I think I'm cured!"

Standing over her cart at row 13, the stewardess dropped a glass full of ice. She swore.

"There are children on board," Dad scolded her, which made both Adam and Molly laugh. His language was worse than anyone's.

The stewardess smiled brightly at them. As she started to mop up the water that was dripping over the edges of the cart, she told all the passengers nearby how very sorry she was.

Another thought suddenly occurred to Molly. "Have you got Granddad safe?" she asked Adam.

Of course! In the panic he'd forgotten all about Granddad.

Adam patted his pocket. "Are you there, Granddad?" He whispered.

"It's a little dark in here," came a voice from inside the pocket.

"Shhshh," hissed Molly. "Quiet, Granddad." Bringing a ghost on a plane must definitely be against every security law in existence.

But he seemed to have made it through the turbulence okay. She turned her attention back to her Dad.

"Are you sure you're all right, Dad? Adam was asking.

He grinned. "I'm fine."

"But not for long." The voice came from behind Dad's seat.

Adam whipped his head around to see who was speaking, but only the stewardess was there. She was getting to her feet and hurrying down the aisle, assuring everyone in her very sweet voice that everything was just fine.

He needed to tell Molly what he had just heard. Because they couldn't take any chances. Not now.

Not with what they knew was coming.